AF291956

We of the Earth:

Stories About Humans

Z.B. Salgado

This is a work of fiction. Names, characters, places, situations and incidents either are the product of the author's imagination or are used fictitiously. Any resemblance to actual persons, living or dead, events, or locales is entirely coincidental.

For my wife, who kept telling me to finish writing
the last few ones.

Even though the really good video games were on
sale during quarantine.

For my parents and my step-dad, you guys
really tried.

For my grandpa who was always there, you will
always be missed.

And finally, for the people who keep saying, "Come
at me, bro," and "I can't even,"

You're welcome.

Contents

ON AND ON

"Is it me, or does it look exactly like a scene from one of those brochures they give us at the annual employee benefits overview?" Ted asked, pulling James' attention from the beautiful white sand beach that sprawled before them.

Even from the airport terminal, the view of the cerulean water was incredible. James slid his eyes from the Jamaican shoreline and looked at his longtime friend and coworker. Ted, his wife Susan, and James' new girlfriend, Rita, were accompanying him on an all-inclusive resort vacation. "I bet they stood in this very spot to take the picture," James offered with a smile before resting his sunglasses on the bridge of his nose.

Working in the airline industry certainly had its benefits, and James was eager to show Rita a good time. She liked shiny things, after all. He knew Ted felt the same about impressing Susan. They'd been in a rough patch for the last year, which is how long ago Susan's unfulfilled desire for Ted to give her a child had reached a breaking point.

"What do you think, babe?" James asked, turning to Rita as she and Susan walked up. She fixated on a broken latch on her suitcase and didn't seem to notice the beach shimmering ahead.

"I think that airline owes me a new bag," she snapped.

Before James could offer a solution, a large shuttle van drove up and blocked the view. Out stepped a large and undeniably attractive man. His biceps pressed against the crisp fabric of his uniform, which bore the logo of the resort where they had reservations.

"Hello, everyone, and welcome to Jamaica! I am Samuel, and I will be your tour guide and first point of contact for all your needs while you stay with us. I will be taking you to the hotel where we'll meet up with the rest of your group. Please hop in the van and leave your bags to me." With a warm smile that had Rita and Susan exchanging glances, Samuel got busy hoisting everyone's bags into the back of the vehicle.

James had his eyes glued out the window, admiring the scenery with each passing mile on the way to the hotel. He listened half-heartedly to Rita's complaints about the flight and her damaged bag. She loudly expressed her doubt that the rest of the trip would go any smoother. James sighed and wondered if her beautiful, pouting mouth was worth the negativity that so often came out of it.

"Here we are!" Samuel announced cheerfully, interrupting James' thoughts and the conversation between the women. "Check in at the desk and make yourself comfortable. The whole group will be meeting in the hotel restaurant in one hour," he advised. Then he jumped out of the van to unload their things.

"How about we go upstairs and I take your mind off that bag?" James offered to Rita, holding her hand and giving it a gentle kiss. He heard Ted laugh at the cheesy line and gesture, but he was in Jamaica and completely unbothered.

Rita eyed him doubtfully. "I'm tired. Why don't we just find a place to sit down here while we wait for dinner to start?"

James knew he'd been outvoted when Susan chimed in, voicing that she also wanted to sit for a minute and take in the view. Ted made no effort to tip the scale in James' favor, so they found seats near the restaurant and waited for the other group members to arrive.

By the time dinner started, their group consisted of the four of them, an older couple from somewhere in Eastern Europe, and an attractive young pair of friends from Australia. Try as he might, James was having a hard time keeping his eyes off the one who had introduced herself as Nadine.

The conversation was light, and the food was delectable. Everyone gave a brief introduction and shared a little about their profession or passions. James felt Rita relax next to him as she sipped her third rum punch. As the sights, sounds, and scents of the beach blew through the seaside restaurant, he had to admit that he was having a pretty good time. Jamaica did not disappoint.

The next morning, the group met on the beach for a lesson in horseback riding. As they walked towards the sand, Ted asked James if he had much experience with horses even though he already knew the answer. "I'm from New York, Ted. Of course, I've never ridden a horse. This seems like a great learning opportunity." The closest he'd ever been to riding one was on the cart it pulled and only for a few minutes.

When everyone had gathered on the beach around Samuel and the eight horses that accompanied him, he began giving a safety overview. Once he'd instructed everyone on how to manage their horse, he peeled off his shirt and gave a demonstration of proper mounting and dismounting. James couldn't ignore the giggling and swooning of all the women in the group when Samuel's bulging pectoral muscles gleamed in the sunlight.

It seemed Ted wasn't immune to Samuel's effect, either. He watched the way the larger man helped Susan onto her horse and felt a spike of jealousy rush through him. "Did you see where he put his hand?" Ted muttered to James.

James had seen it alright. He'd also seen the ripple of pleasure that danced along Susan's shoulders, but he wasn't about to share that with his best friend. "Maybe they're just friendly here in Jamaica," he offered. Ted seemed comforted by this possibility, and he followed the guide's lead on how to mount his horse.

After a long day of riding horseback, James had high expectations for a relaxing dinner with his companions. However, it wasn't long after the appetizers and a few rounds of drinks that Ted couldn't resist bringing up the intimate touch—and later a lingering hug—he had witnessed between his wife and the strapping Jamaican tour guide.

"Did you think I wouldn't see?" he asked, accusation dripping from every word. James tried to gauge how drunk the man was, but it was impossible to know how much alcohol any of them had had with the constant day drinking. It was like an infinite open bar. All their faces were red at this point.

"It's no big deal, Ted," Susan gently tried to reassure him.

It didn't help matters when Rita chimed in with, "Yeah, she's on vacation. She deserves to be touched by a *real man* while she's here." She brought a margarita glass to her pretty lips and pretended she hadn't said anything wrong. One glance at the vein popping on Ted's forehead told James that there was no undoing the damage.

Susan searched for words to diffuse the situation, but even she had to admit her eight-year marriage and zero children added up to some cosmic male deficiency in her husband. As her mouth flapped open and closed with nothing useful to say, Ted excused himself to the bar. With clenched hands, he made his way quickly but carefully across the restaurant patio.

"Good riddance," Rita said with an eyeroll. The alcohol had loosened her up more than usual. "Let's you and I go upstairs and let these two sort things out," she offered, placing a hand high on James' thigh. He glanced at Susan, but she was too busy picking up her things to notice they'd spoken.

James ignored Rita's hand and asked Susan if she was alright. "I'm fine. I will be on the beach if anyone needs me," was her terse reply. With her handbag clamped under her arm, she turned and sauntered away from the restaurant towards the waterfront. James thought he recognized the silhouette of their tour guide against the water.

"Why don't you join her?" James asked, gently removing Rita's hand from his leg and placing it on her own lap. "I'm gonna go make sure Ted's alright. You may have struck a nerve earlier."

Rita didn't try to hide her annoyance. She rolled her eyes again until her long false lashes brushed against her penciled-in eyebrows. "Ugh, fine. But you owe me, leaving me high and dry like this."

James muttered an apology and made his way to the bar to talk to Ted. The kiss he left on Rita's cheek felt like an embarrassment to the discarded woman. Angrily, she followed Susan to the beachfront to vent. No sooner had Rita caught up to her did she notice a glint of silver peeking from Susan's bag. She was sneaking sips from it while gazing out at the water.

"Oh my god, you lush. Is that a flask?" Rita asked, sidling up beside the other woman on the sand. "Can I have some?"

"Be my guest," Susan offered. She watched Rita take a delicate sip of the gin before realizing how high quality it was. She tossed back a little more. "I can't believe those jerks. This is the most boring vacation I've ever been on. So what if I want to have a little fun with a local?"

"Did Samuel really touch your ass?" Rita asked, handing back the flask.

As if conjured by the mention of his name, the women noticed Samuel and another man walking towards them from down the shore. "You bet he did, and he's going to do it again. Here he comes," Susan said with a glint in her eye. She stood and began waving wildly.

"Samuel! Hello! It's me and Rita. Come over here, won't you?"

The large man smiled back, the fading sunset catching his teeth and making them shine. "Susan, lovely to see you. My friend Thomas and I are taking an evening walk." They stopped a good one hundred feet away and were just out of earshot when Rita whispered to Susan.

"This is a bad idea, Susie. You're only having an argument with Ted…"

The other woman didn't seem to hear her. "Come on, boys. I've got a top-shelf gin here. We'd love to get to know you better."

Rita hissed her friend's name, as if she could call Susan back from the ledge of infidelity she was tip-toeing around. As soon as Samuel and Thomas approached, smelling of coconut oil and pheromones and the ocean—looking every bit as delicious as they were forbidden—Rita suddenly forgot all about her own loyalty to James.

Back at the bar, James was doing a poor job of consoling his friend. It seemed the more drinks he bought him, the deeper Ted sunk into despondency and self-loathing. While he moaned on and on about what a hard time Susan gave him for not yet impregnating her, James cast his eyes lazily around the bar. He spotted Nadine from the tour group and couldn't deny the surge of adrenaline that pulsed through him.

"Look alive, Ted. We have company," James said under his breath as Nadine and her attractive friend Kat approached them.

"Good evening, boys," Kat purred, placing a hand on Ted's back, still hunched over his drink. The touch sent a jolt through him, and his demeanor changed almost instantly. Though the puffy eyes and swollen nose were harder to dispel.

Before the Australian women could jump to conclusions about Ted's appearance, James set the record straight. "The women were a bit rough on ol' Ted here. Nothing I have said seems to help. You two don't have any advice for an aching heart, do you?"

Kat and Nadine clicked their tongues and made reassuring noises as they flanked Ted on either side. They asked him to share his woes with them. James made room for Nadine to sidle up beside him. He remained a perfect gentleman while her curvy, tan hip pressed against his thigh. The heat coming off her skin reminded him of the scorching Australian desert, and he took a long, cooling sip of his Moscow mule.

Without emasculating himself too much, Ted briefly explained what the last eight years had been like with Susan and how deeply the comments had hurt him. When he asked Kat whether he should read into the exchanges he'd witnessed between his wife and Samuel, she laughed it off.

"I think you're overreacting," she said. "Considering the setting, it's normal for an American woman to let a little attention from the locals go to her head."

Nadine chimed in, adding, "Sometimes it's not enough to bring a girl to paradise. You gotta pamper her, too. Make her feel like a queen."

As if her words flicked a switch in him, Ted pushed himself away from the bar and began walking with renewed intention towards the hotel gift shop. As James stood up to follow him, he felt Nadine lean into him once again. She looked at him over her shoulder, through suggestively lowered eyelids. A glance at Kat revealed she wore a similar expression.

"If things don't work out with him and Susan, let him know I'm in room three-eleven," she said in her perfect Australian accent, accompanied by a wink before taking another slow drink.

"Thanks for your help, ladies," James said genuinely. He placed a hand on the middle of Nadine's back and added, "I'm sure we'll see you again soon," before he rushed off to make sure Ted was staying out of trouble.

At the hotel gift shop, Ted had selected a bouquet of twenty-four deep red roses for Susan. He was looking around for chocolates or some sort of stuffed animal when James caught up to him. "What's the plan here?" he asked, keeping criticism out of his voice.

Ted was clearly drunk, but he was determined in his mission. "I give her the roses, she realizes that I see her pain, and that I am here for her, no matter what…" He trailed off, his fingers absently caressing the velvet of a single rose petal.

"Right, then I should get a bouquet for Rita, as well." James selected a more modest dozen roses in red and white, and the two men made their purchases. It wasn't until they were standing at the exit of the gift shop that they realized they had no idea where their women had gone.

"It's late. Maybe we should check the rooms," Ted suggested.

James wasn't quite so optimistic that their ladies had called it an early night. "Last I heard, they were bound for the beach if I remember correctly. Let's take a walk out there before we go upstairs." Ted seemed to like the idea of fresh air, and the two friends took off for the waterfront with flowers in hand.

Ted heard the moaning before he could see anything. The smell of coconut oil and Susan's perfume caused a knot to form in the pit of his stomach. The drunk man fumbled in his pocket for his phone, which wasn't good for much so far out of range of the hotel WiFi. He silently rushed to activate the phone's flashlight feature. He shone it in the crevices of the rocks, hoping to find two young teens and not his wife of almost a decade.

As the beam of light slid over the jumble of white and brown limbs, he realized he was witnessing not only Susan in the throes of infidelity, but Rita as well! The two women were sandwiched between Samuel and what appeared to be a younger, thinner version of him. All four of them were in various stages of undress, and Ted couldn't help the well of tears that sprang to his eyes.

"I don't *believe* this!" he cried, throwing the bouquet of flowers at Susan's feet right as James finally caught up to him. As the four deceivers scrambled to cover their exposed parts, James tried to make sense of what he was only seeing in snippets, due to Ted's flailing flashlight. His friend's mounting sobs told him everything. As the drunken cuckold begin ambling back towards the hotel, James decided he wasn't letting Samuel or his friend off quite that easily. He rolled up the cuffs of his shirt and stepped towards the men, who were now on their feet in the rock alcove.

"Don't do anything stupid, James!" Rita cried just as James took a forceful swing at the smaller man.

Unfortunately, Thomas was a fighter by passion, and he bobbed deftly out of the way of James' hurtling fist. The sound of his knuckles smashing into the rock was enough to turn everyone's stomach. As James wailed in pain, Samuel tried to calm him down with assurances like, "They called us over. We all drank so much. We were only having fun. Please understand this was not a slight against you or Ted…"

James couldn't hear anything over the pain in his hand and the blood that was rage-pounding in his ears. He'd taken such good care of Rita, and this was how she showed her gratitude! In a flurry of embarrassment and pain, James made sure to stomp on both discarded bouquets as he marched back to the hotel, following Ted's footsteps the whole way.

To the girls' credit, or discredit in this case, they showed up at James' hotel room door within minutes of the incident. Ted, in all his grief and self-pity, had been sure that Susan would spend the night in Samuel's arms. But now she was banging at the door alongside Rita, trying to explain away her behavior as a drunken mistake.

"Should I let them in?" James asked, pressing a makeshift ice pack onto his aching knuckles.

Ted held his head in his hands, overwhelmed by the alcohol and emotions that were controlling his every move. "I don't know. After everything, I don't think this was a one-off. Susan has been cheating on me for years, for all I know."

James took a mental inventory of everything he knew about Susan and Ted's relationship. Even he couldn't deny the likelihood that Ted was right. His thoughts soon veered to Rita, who was guilty of the same indiscretion. James wondered if he could ever slip his hands under her dress again after having seen Thomas doing the very same thing.

"I'm going to tell them to get lost," James said decisively before crossing the room and whipping open the door. "Get away from this room before I call security on you both," he barked.

The smeared makeup and disheveled hair was not a good look for either of the crying women. Rita tried to protest, "It was a stupid mistake! We let the alcohol go to our heads. It didn't mean anything!"

James only gave her a dark look before closing the door in her face. In a matter of minutes, he had gathered all Rita's belongings and stuffed them into her broken suitcase. He said nothing as he opened the door once again and dropped the bag heavily on the floor.

The following morning, both men were nursing serious hangovers and an equally serious feeling of heartache. As James downed three ibuprofen and took a large drink from the hotel-provided water bottle, he couldn't help noticing how enticing the sea looked outside the room window. If there was anything he and his buddy needed this morning, it was a heart to heart on the water.

"What do you say we go fishing today?" James asked the moment he heard Ted wander into the kitchenette to put on coffee.

Ted rubbed a hand over his face. As the coffee maker began sputtering out the hot black holy water, Ted agreed it sounded like a good way to take his mind off the night before. An hour later, the two men were pushing away from shore in a little rowboat loaded with bait and tackle, a cooler of Red Stripe, and a portable radio playing classic rock.

"What a trip," James mused when they'd gotten a good distance from the land.

"Tell me about it," Ted agreed, taking a bottle from the cooler and offering another to James.

As they both popped the cap off their beverage, James felt a sudden melancholy threatening to take over his mind. All the dreams and visions he'd had of building a future with Rita were blowing away on the Jamaican breeze. He took a sip and began swishing it around on his tongue as Ted broke the silence with similar musings of his own.

"It's incredible to watch almost a decade of history with someone completely disappear." He took a long drink from his beer.

"I can't imagine, Ted. I have to apologize for bringing along such a bad example. I don't honestly think Susan would have done what she did without goading from Rita. I've known she was bad news for a while, but how do I say no to a mouth like that?"

Ted laughed dryly. "No, I don't think Rita is wholly to blame. Susan has been wanting to cheat on me for years. I found a journal she was keeping a long time ago. I guess I've been in denial ever since."

James shook his head. "You deserve better. We both do." He leaned back on his elbows, took another slow slug of his beer, and waited until he felt a tug on the end of his line. Nearly an hour had passed in silence when the men noticed movement on the shore.

At first glance, it was clear the two people on the beach were women. Both men let their rigidity subside when they realized the women weren't Susan and Rita but Kat and Nadine. They were wearing barely-there bikini tops paired with ultra-short shorts. They looked more appealing than an Outback steak. James didn't even need to say a word. A single glance at Ted's eager expression was all the invitation he needed to take the boat back to land.

The two Australian women looked positively delighted to see Ted and

James. "What excellent timing to find you here!" Kat said when the boat collided with the sand and they were close enough to climb on.

"We're only pretending to fish," Ted said with a level of good humor that surprised James. "Care to join us?"

Kat and Nadine put together the context clues and realized that the attempt at making up with their ladies had not gone according to plan. "As long as you're *actually* drinking, I'm in," Nadine said with a laugh before tossing her bag at James' feet.

The two beautiful women stepped on board, and James rowed them back out to sea. While his strong shoulders propelled the oars through the water, he listened to Kat tell Ted a story about her worst breakup. Their charming accents and the way their tan skin glittered in the afternoon sun were mesmerizing.

While something had undoubtedly been lost on the sandy shores of Jamaica, James and Ted couldn't help believing that something equally beautiful had been gained. They felt at peace in the company of these women, who wanted nothing from them but a few brews and a laugh. With the warm white sun gleaming above and the clear blue waves lapping against their vessel, they'd finally found their version of paradise.

THE LONG WAY HOME

I woke up to the sound of my roommate humming holiday music while wrapping gifts, and of course, he was recording himself with his phone again so that he could post it on YouTube later. A very ambitious dude, I thought. He kept hoping that someday his humming cover of "Rudolf the Red Nosed Reindeer", along with other great songs he butchered, would somehow gain over a million views and make him famous. The poor guy checked his own videos everyday just to raise the views.

"Sorry, did I wake you?" he asked, continuing to wrap his presents, now changing his song to "Here Comes Santa Claus."

I sat up gradually. My eyes were still trying to catch up with my surroundings. "Nope, it's fine," I said groggily. "Had to wake up anyways." I always tried to restrain myself when lashing out on him, due to the fact that I would be living with this poor soul for the rest of the school year. Bad PR between roommates would just create a hazardous environment.

My alarm rang a few seconds after. A nice little gift from a friend that I just couldn't throw away, even though my phone had an alarm feature on it. The mechanical screaming started, just as it did every morning during my stay in this academic prison I call a dorm room. I took my sweet time before I smacked the snooze button, hoping profoundly that the noise would make him stop humming, but he continued like nothing happened.

Though it was already past seven, it was dark and dreary outside. It was a big change for me since I was used to California weather. Washington was a bit of a challenge to adjust to. Though it wasn't as hot during the summer, the winter was a lot colder than I was used to.

I quickly retreated to the bathroom and hopped into the shower, the cold drops of water dripping down on my face, waking me up instantly and drowning the intense humming in the other room at the same time.

After showering, I pushed a slab of toothpaste out of its container and caught it on my toothbrush. I found myself looking at my clone in the other side of the mirror, brushing my teeth for a few minutes. "Well not bad," I complimented myself vainly.

My roommate was already gone when I got out. He might've said goodbye while I was in the shower, or he might have just left. We were never very close, just sharing the space. But I was relieved that the humming had stopped for now. I quickly put on my jeans, a plain white shirt, and my $19.99 red school hoodie.

I found myself walking in a very silent hallway. A lot of the dorm rooms were already empty. Most of the students left early to go home for the holidays or to go on a trip somewhere with their friends. I was a bit envious of those who went on trips; they escaped the gift giving madness at home and managed to have a lot of fun at the same time. Those of us who were going home had to spend a week or more thinking of what to give to our family members and feeling guilty about the ones we couldn't afford to buy gifts for.

There were only four people in my class out of the twenty-seven that were supposed to be there. They were probably out having fun somewhere. My envy grew even more when our skimpy looking TA walked into the class, announcing that our professor had left for the holidays and that class was cancelled. "Great," I sighed. "Just great." Though I did find a little comfort in seeing the same look on my other classmates' faces. At least I didn't suffer this terrible ordeal on my own. This kind of academic torture was common in college. Professors would use their paid leave and sick days to extend their vacations, but who could blame them, right? Any professor would want the opportunity to extend his time away from the students. They could be somewhat… bothersome. At almost every test I had taken, there was usually a student or two who failed or got a low grade, and they usually approached the teacher in hopes of retaking the test or doing extra credit work. The exams were generally easy. Did the public-school system fail them? When they implemented the *No Child Left Behind* program in high school and elementary, it didn't work for everyone, it seems. They were left behind. And every time that happened, the professors had to pretend to sympathize with them.

I quickly fled from the scene, falling back to my dorm room to pack my things. My flight wasn't until early tomorrow morning; I scheduled it to give myself just enough time to pack after class was over and to park my car safely in the parking garage, so I could take the bus to the airport. If I knew I would be free by now, I could've already left for California.

It didn't take me long to pack my things. One suitcase was enough for me. After all, I still had a lot of clothes at my parent's house. I made some time to clean up the place a little, just to feel at ease. All that was left was for me to do was to move my car, so it would be safer while I was gone. My stomach suddenly growled. I had forgotten to feed it breakfast. Good thing I was the only one in the room; if someone else was in there, they probably would have thought that an alien life form would burst out of me after hearing that.

I made my way to the cafeteria before my stomach complained even more. I slowly looked over the limited selection of "gourmet food" that they offered. I was being eyeballed by one of the cafeteria workers as she walked around in her plastic apron and what looked like a shower cap on her head. I couldn't stop myself from chuckling a little. I found a bit of humor in our country's food prices. A good-sized hamburger was priced at $2.99 and a regular Caesar Salad was priced at a hefty $4.99.

"Glad to know the system is very supportive of our dietary needs," I muttered under my breath, as I grabbed the salad. I chomped it down to the last leaf. After my stomach seemed satisfied, I slowly trotted my way to the parking lot to move my car.

Before I could even get out of the cafeteria, my cellphone started to buzz. There was a slight vibration in my pocket. "Might be the President," I said to myself. I slowly reached for it and gazed at the image of the caller on my phone. It was Elise, the girl I've wanted to go out with since high school. When I thought everything was going well, she just deleted me from her life without a reason. I know it's a cliché, but she was the one, the one that got away. I took a deep breath and hit the green phone button on my keypad.

"Jack?" her voice said from inside my phone. It was the same as it used to be. Though there was a bit of urgency in her voice.

"Yes?" I replied immediately. We haven't spoken for over three years. "Who is this?" I pretended.

"It's Elise," she paused briefly. "I know we haven't talked in a while, but I really need your help."

It took a while to sink in; a girl I haven't seen or heard from in a long while suddenly comes back as a distressed damsel. I slowly collected myself. "What happened? Is everything okay?" I asked.

"Are you still at your school right now?" she asked, sounding hopeful.

"Yes, though I'm leaving tomorrow morning to go back home."

"Thank goodness!" she cheered over the phone. When her excitement died down, she started to talk again. "I know it's sudden, but can you do me favor and pick me up? I'm at the mall near your school; I'll fill you in with the details when we meet. Please, please, please," she pleaded.

A myriad of thoughts ran through my head, and before I knew it, I was debating with myself. It was a fierce battle. One that should have been remembered as the most grueling man versus himself conflict; had the other side won…I persuaded myself that this was a necessity. Somehow, her phone call had dug up some buried feelings, and I wanted to see what I could find. Within a few moments, I suddenly found myself turning the keys in the ignition and driving towards the direction of the mall.

"I'm here. Where are you?" I asked in a text message. A few seconds later, my phone buzzed.

"I am at the coffee shop on the second floor," she replied.

My legs automatically headed for the escalator. Since this particular mall was the only mall within twenty miles of our school, it was a popular place for students. It was also the only place with a movie theater, a place I considered sacred and dedicated most of my Saturdays to.

I found her waiting for me at a table outside the coffee shop. She was wearing a blue winter jacket, a nice pair of jeans (which fitted her nicely by the way), along with her winter boots and a scarf. Her long, silky black hair, just as I remembered, was hanging freely on her shoulders. Beside her were a small green suitcase and a small cup. The years have been more than kind to her. If anything, she looked a lot prettier than I last saw her. She smiled and waved at me as I approached her.

"Jack!" She stood up and hugged me. I felt like a war veteran coming home to his wife after being deployed.

"Elise, nice to see you again," I said as I returned her hug.

We sat down, waiting for the excitement of our reunion to go down a notch.

"So, what brings you here? You sounded a little distraught on the phone," I started. She looked at me and studied my face for a while before she talked. There it was. I caught her gaze as I looked back at her. Her enticing brown eyes, the ones that had once taken hold of me years ago, were beginning to grip at me again.

"I actually came here with my boyfriend—well, ex-boyfriend—to visit his uncle who lives near here. But we had a big fight here in the mall, and he started yelling at me," she said, almost sobbing. "I've been planning to end it for a while. He wasn't really treating me well, but him yelling at me was the last straw."

Mixed emotions began whirling up inside me. I was actually a little upset. I lied earlier; I actually had a faint idea why she stopped talking to me. Right before we ceased communicating with each other, she would always call me and text me. She would often talk to me about her boyfriend, which was a somewhat painful topic, considering I had feelings for her. But I had to be a good friend to her; it was the only role I had since that overbearing, controlling, sorry excuse for a human being took the boyfriend position. I never met the guy, but the way she described him made him sound like a complete jerk.

One thing I could never forget was when I sent her a text message saying we should go out on a date and watch a movie. She asked me to send the text message again. I did, only to realize later that her boyfriend had somehow gotten a hold of her phone, and she wasn't the one I had texted. I guess that made him pretty upset. He probably asked her to delete me from her phone and never talk to me again. Not long after that, my text messages and phone calls were no longer answered; she even deleted me from Facebook. I stopped trying; I could take a hint. I was practical enough to know when I was not wanted. But I always hated the fact that she obeyed him. In a way, I guess I really hated the fact that she chose him over me. Though I didn't really convey my feelings to her at the time, I never did.

"Is that the same guy you used to complain to me about back then? The guy you always suspected of cheating?" I asked.

"Yes. I don't know what came over me back then. I was in denial," she said, looking down.

"Well, I've said my piece about him before. I always thought of him as a complete jerk. A lucky jerk, considering he went out with you," I said.

"I'm sorry," she said softly. She was almost teary-eyed. I couldn't really blame her. Sometimes, how we feel about someone can change us, make us do things that we don't want just to keep that someone close, just to be with them.

"Anyways, what was the big emergency?" I asked, slowly quelling the anger inside of me.

"Since my ex and I drove here, I kind of lost my ride home," she said. "So, I checked online to book a flight to California instead. But everything is fully booked for the next three days," she paused briefly.

"Here's the pitch," I said inside my head.

"So, I was wondering if I can hitch a ride with you, since you're going there."

I had a feeling that something like that would happen. Obviously, I had already booked a flight for the next day. But she somehow thought I was driving home. To even consider the possibility of wasting a non-refundable ticket just to take her home was insane. Not to mention, the hours and hours of driving time and gas money I would spend. "It's not worth it; you should just walk away right now. You're just being used," I said in my head. "If you don't do it, she's going to plead with her boyfriend to take her home, probably make up with him in the process, and they'll be together again. This might be your only chance," I argued. It was an enticing idea, but in the end, it was similar to a situation where you would find something you really liked in a store, but as soon as you checked the price tag, you walk away. That was how I felt.

At that exact moment, my phone buzzed. When they say, "Lightning doesn't strike the same place twice," they were lying. I was struck and struck again the minute I answered that phone. Normally, I wouldn't entertain phone calls from numbers I didn't recognize. But the situation called for a time out. I didn't have that candy bar that they eat on TV when they need a break, so the phone call was my only alternative.

"Give me a minute. I have to take this call," I said and walked a few steps away from the table. She nodded and watched me as I went.

"Hello, Sir. My name is Juliette, and I'm from the airline. I'm afraid I have bad news," said the woman in an apologetic tone.

"Lay it on me," I said idly.

"Sir, I'm afraid your flight has been delayed. We detected some engine problems on the plane, and it's not going to be done by tomorrow morning. The next flight we can get you on is the day after tomorrow with upgraded seating."

"Of course, someone is playing cupid up there, and they are a pretty good shot," I said in my head.

"Sir?" she repeated.

"Is it possible to get a refund from this?" I asked to finalize my pre-determined destiny.

"Yes, we can actually give you a full refund," she said.

That was it. It was a sign from the heavens, this wasn't meant to be. In a biblical sense, I was the Jacob, and this was my trial. "Old man, you got me. Your will be done," I said to myself.

"I'll just take the refund then," I said calmly.

"We'll do that right away, sir. Sorry again for the inconvenience."

"It's okay. It's not your fault." It really wasn't. I ended the call and turned back to Elise.

"Well, Elise, looks like you and I are going on a road trip," I said as I walked back to our table.

Her face lit up with joy. She suddenly jumped from her table and hugged me again. "Yay! Thank you!" she exclaimed. I grabbed her suitcase, and we marched our way towards my car.

It was a quick trip to the student housing area. I still couldn't believe that I was in this situation. The probability and timing of it all was just as rigged as professional sports.

"I'm just going to get my things from my room. Do you want to come with or do you want stay here?" I asked.

"I'll go," she said and opened the door. We made our way to the dormitories and into my room. I praised myself for cleaning up earlier. There wasn't a lot of furniture to look at, just the two beds, our small kitchen, and the bathroom. She sat down on my bed while I put together the things I was taking. I had to pack an extra bag for the road trip. She slowly pushed herself back to lie down. She looked really comfortable. I imagined myself being in that small twin bed with her. It wasn't a bad image. Yes, I'm a guy. Then I dismissed the thought and continued to focus on packing.

"Do you remember the first day we met?" she asked suddenly.

"Yes," I replied. It wasn't something I could easily forget. I pictured myself, back in my senior year of high school. I was helping the school, guiding people in the parking lot and showing them where to sit. My high school self, wearing my JROTC (Junior Reserve Officer's Training Corps) uniform for a school football game. I saw two new faces in uniform like me, serving food near the bleachers, and I somehow unconsciously walked up to them. One of them really caught my attention… That was probably the only time I would've said yes if I was asked if I believed in love at first sight.

"You came up to me out of nowhere, and you said, excuse me miss, I don't think we've been properly introduced," she said it just as I remembered. "Why did you do that?" She sat up and asked me.

I really didn't have an answer to that. Perhaps, I just found her attractive. Though I have met a lot of other attractive girls before, I can't really say I've done that particular scenario on anyone else that way. At that moment, looking at her, I had felt like someone else.

"I really don't know. It was like my body just automatically walked up to you," I said. Which was true, it really did in a way. I didn't even plan it. Usually I give myself a quick little rehearsal speech in my head before saying something to someone, but that time was different.

"You were so cheesy. After that, you gave me your phone and told me to put my number in. 'In case you have any questions about the program or if you need anything,' I believe you said something along those lines," she smirked. "But it was the other way around; you should've put your number in my phone instead of me putting mine in yours."

"Yeah, I might have been a little nervous," I said, sardonically.

I ran that memory in my head like it was yesterday. I remembered her putting her number in my phone. It felt like I won some sort of victory. From then on, we started texting and calling each other, and eventually, we spent some time together after school.

"You kept sending me funny pickup lines," she said laughing.

"I did not!" I defended, immediately denying it. But I was pretty sure I did. I actually almost convinced myself that I had strong feelings for her.

"The first line you ever used on me was 'Are you tired?' and I asked why, and you said 'Because you've been running in my head all day.'" She teased. "Cheese muffin!"

She used to call me that whenever I tried to do something slightly romantic or if I did some sort of small comedic relief.

"Alright, let's go," I said after I was done putting my things together.

Before we left my dorm room, we mapped out our trip and planned our stops. The last thing we needed was a fully booked inn when we needed to stop and rest. It was about eighteen hours of driving, non-stop. But I would never put myself in that kind of position. Even if I had to spend extra money, I booked us in two inns along the way. She told me that her douche bag of an ex-boyfriend was a cheapskate and drove non-stop, taking turns all the way. This caused him to drive off the road a few times because he was too sleepy to drive.

"What an idiot," I muttered.

I had done a fair deal of long-range driving myself, so I knew what it felt like to be driving for hours and hours. At some point, exhaustion would come and catch you off-guard. Being alert and prepared on the road was a matter of life and death. Besides the weather, road construction, and other unforeseen circumstances, we had to share the road with incompetent drivers, and it didn't help if you were sleep deprived. She was a little uncomfortable with sharing a room at first, so I booked the rooms with two beds to give ourselves some personal space. I consider myself a gentleman, after all. With that, I sealed the deal.

Even though we hadn't been together in a while, it wasn't hard for us to get reacquainted with each other. It was almost like we just picked up where we left off.

Before we left, we stopped by a big parking lot where an old man standing in front of a Goodwill Container greeted us. It was a part of my yearly routine to give away old clothes and such to charity.

"At least Santa can't say I was bad all year," I said jokingly to the old man as I handed him a bag full of things. Elise laughed as I sped out of the parking lot.

It was almost noon when we got on the road. The radio stations were filled with static. I didn't really get the chance to burn some songs on a disc, and I lost my music player somehow, so the only other source of music in the car were my old mixed CD's, stowed away in the glove compartment, waiting to be called into action again. The first CD we found was a mixture of Backstreet Boys, Spice Girls, and a bunch of other 90s music, which we surprisingly still knew the lyrics to. After what seemed like an hour long jamming session, complete with hand gestures, we finally got bored of them and moved on to the next CD.

The next one was composed of Boyz II Men, R. Kelly, and Usher. She surprised me by rapping R. Kelly's "Ignition (Remix)." She was pretty good at it too.

"Whew, watch out, Eminem!" I teased.

The last song on the CD was Usher's "Nice and Slow", which was a bit nostalgic for me. I guess she remembered it too when it came on.

"Oo! This song!" she exclaimed. "Remember?"

It was our song. During spring break, we went on a school trip, a sort of camp I guess you could say. One night, they organized a small dinner and dance night for all the students. It was a little awkward since I don't really label myself as someone who can dance. I had the grace and coordination of a three-legged baby elephant. But when that song came on, Elise suddenly grabbed me and took me to the dance floor, and we slow danced to it. I recall feeling so dumb back then because I hadn't even heard or known anything about that song until that moment. It was one of the longest few minutes of slow dancing in my life. I wanted time to freeze, while we were holding each other just like that. But eventually, the music stopped. It always does.

"I remember. We danced to this at camp," I said, gingerly reminiscing through that memory.

"Aw, you remembered!" she said smiling.

"I have a confession to make," I said suddenly. I tried to stop myself, but I already blurted it out.

"What is it?" she asked, poised. She was ready for anything.

"On the way to camp," I started, "while we were on the 'Big Yellow Twinkie' as you called it…" Which was what she called our school buses. She nodded and motioned for me to continue.

"We were sitting next to each other; I was just pretending to be asleep when you were holding my head on your lap. I even overheard someone tease you about me being your boyfriend, and I waited for you to push me off or wake me up, but you didn't," I said dramatically. I was anxious to know what her response was. I even started to sweat a little.

She looked calm still, and it didn't take her long to respond. "Wow. So sly," she said. "I really thought you were asleep, and I didn't want to wake you. But I really didn't mind too much."

I laughed. That was a little better than I thought, but she still seemed surprised by it. "I thought it was pretty slick."

"It was. Good move," she said, giving off a faint smile.

The whole time, we were just going through old memories. All of a sudden, the sun went down and night had taken over. Before I knew it, we had already reached our first inn. Since we started the trip a little late in the day, we decided to stop in Eugene, Oregon. Within a few minutes after checking in, we carried our bags up the elevator and into our room. It was a nice, cozy place. There were two beds, just as I asked. There was also a bathroom, a small refrigerator, and a bulky looking TV set.

I was tired. But being the considerate person that I was, I drove all the way there by myself and just let her relax comfortably in the passenger's seat. I asked her if she wanted to take a shower, but she told me to go ahead and use it first.

I invaded the bathroom and turned on the shower. I stood there for a while as the hot water massaged my body. It almost seemed like my fatigue was being washed away. When I got out, she was already sound asleep. She didn't even have a chance to put the blanket on, and it was a little chilly in our room, so I took my own blanket off my bed and put it on her. As I finished laying it down, my hand accidentally brushed her pillow. It was a little wet.

I was no detective, but when I saw her cellphone in her hand, I put two and two together. She had it off the whole trip there, but she probably turned it on while I was in the shower. Her ex-boyfriend must have left her a bunch of text messages and voicemails, saying how sorry he was about what happened and how he wanted her back, something along those lines. I was a guy too, so I knew how it worked. I had seen how far people were willing to go for those they have feelings for. I'd heard of a guy back in my high school who started yelling outside my best friend's house, a little intoxicated, at four o' clock in the morning. I didn't exactly know what happened, but that was not the way to get into someone's good graces. To me, it was rather stupid. A sleep deprived parent in that neighborhood could have fired a warning shot just to shut him up, but he was alive, and he got the girl back, so I guess it worked. I wasn't in any position to judge though. I was going out of my way to take home a girl that I hadn't spoken to in years. I guess I just hated the fact that, like a lot of girls, she might actually forgive him and take him back. I was starting to think that being a jerk was an attractive quality that girls wanted in a guy. If it were me in her shoes, I wouldn't take that idiot back even if he brought five pounds of government cheese with him.

When I woke up the next morning, Elise was already dressed and ready to go. "Good morning, sleepy head," she said.

"Morning," I replied groggily. I immediately went to the bathroom to brush my teeth and change. She was waiting for me outside.

"Thanks for the blanket last night, by the way. That was nice of you," she said while we walked towards the elevator.

"Yeah, no problem," I said merrily.

Once we got downstairs, we helped ourselves to the inn's "Continental Breakfast," a term that I hadn't quite come to terms with. It was somewhat misleading to me for some reason. When the word "Continental" came to mind, I always pictured a variety of food from all over the continent. Almost like a buffet, I guess. But what they had was a bunch of croissants, wheat bread, cereal, oatmeal, juices and some fruit. I guess they only plowed through a certain part of the continent. Since it was supposedly "free" food, I gave up my inner protest.

After we checked out, we were on the road the again. We drove out of there like we stole the car. Before we knew it, we were almost out of Oregon.

There hadn't been a single cop on the road ever since we left. Which was weird, but it was strangely comforting. After we had stopped at a nearby rest stop, Elise insisted that she drive until the next inn. I didn't stop her. It was a strange feeling that she was able to drive now. I was always the one who did the driving. I glanced at her from the passenger seat from time to time, not saying anything. She smiled. I think she caught me a few times, but she didn't seem to mind. It felt nice being with her. I didn't want to be anywhere else. What I felt with her wasn't exactly the "First thing I think about when I wake up in the morning was her and last thing on my mind before I went to bed was her" kind of feeling, but rather I felt like everyone else I was with before was wrong for me.

I woke up when we got to the freeway exit. I guess I must have fallen asleep. "Hey, we're almost there," she said. "But I'm really hungry. Would you mind if we stopped somewhere to eat?"

"Nope. I'm actually a little hungry myself," I said.

We found a little place on the road. It was some sort of steak house.

"My name is Eva, and I'll be serving you today," said the perky waitress that appeared near our table. "Can I get you guys something to drink?"

"I'll just have water please," I said. Anything else wasn't appealing to me for some reason.

"I'll have the same," said Elise. I guess she wasn't feeling it either. She seemed like she had a lot on her mind.

Eva came back a few minutes later with our drinks and took our orders.

After waiting for a while, she returned and placed a ten-ounce sirloin steak in front of me.

Elise got some sort of shrimp pasta. I didn't even realize how hungry I was until I ate the whole USDA approved beef that landed on our table. Elise also chowed down on her meal. I was pretty sure we could've won one of those small-town pie-eating contests if we somehow ended up in one before we found this place. After we ate, Elise insisted that she pay for at least her portion food, but I told her not to worry about it. "At least she offered," I thought. I've been on several dates, and even though

I make it a rule to always pay, I thought it was a nice gesture to offer or take out their wallet. Some people don't even try.

When I walked up to the "Cashier" sign, it felt kind of odd. The guy behind the desk just took my money and gave me change out of his own pocket. They didn't even have a cash register. But the food was great, so I didn't give it much thought. After a few minutes, we were back on the road again.

"Something bothering you?" I finally asked. Since this morning, Elise seemed really preoccupied. She tried to hide it, but she was never really good at it.

She started to look at me and then looked straight ahead. "I just had some things on my mind, that's all. But I won't let it ruin our trip."

I wanted to press further, but I felt like it would make the remainder of our journey together a little somber.

We continued to drive for a while; it didn't take long for us to reach our final inn in a city called Coalinga. The place we stayed at looked pretty decent and well-maintained, but when we walked in, we suddenly felt a weird vibe.

The innkeeper was a mean looking lady. She gave us a really strange look as we checked in and was shaking her head at us.

"What was that all about?" said Elise as we went on the elevator.

"She probably thought we eloped or something," I said and followed up with a short snicker. She laughed and pressed the button to our floor.

The room was pretty much an almost exact photocopy of the previous one. A generic hotel room with the same stuff as the rest of them. I opened the drawer and left my wallet and keys right next to the King James Bible that was already there.

"I'm going first this time," she said and made her way to the bathroom.

"Alright, do you want me to join you?" I said jokingly

She let out a small laugh and said, "Maybe next time."

I texted my parents and told them that I'd be home tomorrow. They were quick to reply and tell me that they were excited to see me. I turned on the TV while waiting for her to get out of the shower. "This is getting weird," I told myself as I stumbled upon a nostalgic movie while channel surfing. It was a movie called *Juno*, the first movie we watched together. Now I was fully convinced that this was some sort of divine intervention. I watched it for a while, allowing the nostalgia to consume me. It got worse when they started singing *Anyone Else But You*, a song that we used to sing to each other a lot. Somehow, I felt a little sad. Even though we were only a door away from each other, it felt like there was an invisible wall between us.

She came out of the shower in her PJs. "Your turn," she said and jumped onto her bed. I slowly made my way to the shower with my night clothes in tow. It was a quick shower. After I brushed my teeth, I put my clothes on and returned to my bed. I thought she would be asleep again, since she had been driving for a while. But she was still watching TV, the same movie I was watching earlier.

"You were watching this and you didn't tell me?" she said, putting aside the remote on the table. She must have taken it from my bed while I was in the shower.

"Yeah, it's just an old movie," I told her.

She suddenly moved next to me on my bed. "Scoot over," she said. "I can see the TV better from your side of the room."

I quickly gave her some space, and we sat together. We tore through a bag of chips and a pack of cookies before the movie was over. Somehow, we ended up holding each other's hands. Though she was already sleeping when the credits rolled. I was miraculously able to turn off the TV and the overhead light without letting go of her hand or waking her up before I fell asleep. I was watching her sleep beside me for a bit. She seemed like she belonged there. Next to me. For a few minutes, I imagined that I could get used to this, if this was what the future held. Perhaps we could both be happy.

When I woke, she was gone. I heard water running in the bathroom, so she was probably already putting her make-up on. I quickly changed clothes and put all my stuff away. Elise already had all her things ready.

She opened the door a few minutes later, emerging with a curling iron in her hand. "Get ready, mister. I'm getting hungry again," she said.

I laughed at her remark. "Good morning to you too," I managed to say and then quarantined myself in the bathroom. After I brushed my teeth, she went back inside the bathroom to finish up. When we were ready, we went downstairs for another round of "Continental Breakfast."

We took to the streets again and onto the freeway. After going through my mixed CDs one more time, we finally decided to try the local stations. Thank the heavens; the radio stations in California were actually playing some decent music. We spent our last hours together talking about what we had been doing for the past few years, gossiping about our friends, and making cheesy comments to each other. We were almost home.

When we were less than an hour away from her house, I merged into a familiar freeway. It reawakened some dark memories; well, I consider them funny now. Just a few minutes from where we were was where I got pulled over and ticketed for the first and hopefully last time. It was barely four years ago; Elise and my friend Christina were at my house. It was a popular hangout spot back in the day, since it was close to school and always well-stocked with food. Somehow, the three of us got bored and started watching a bunch of "adult movies" from my uncle's collection. Christina and I were no longer minors. Elise, however, was still a few months shy of eighteen. So, I did feel a little guilty for letting her watch it with us.

Later that night, I decided to have a small drinking party. My friends Sandy and Britt came over and drank with us. Again, I should've stopped her, but Elise drank with us too. She did seem like she had problems about something or someone before she went to my house. I don't quite remember what happened then, but later that night, Christina, Britt and Sandy decided to leave and go clubbing. I had to take Elise home before midnight because that was usually when her dad got home. We both drank a little too much that night, though my driving didn't seem to be impaired. We made our way to the freeway entrance, but just after we turned, I saw sirens behind us.

"Oh crap, we are so screwed," said Elise. She took out her phone, probably telling her friends about our situation.

"It's okay. We'll be fine," I assured her, in hopes of calming her down. I knew that I didn't do anything wrong. But somehow, it didn't feel right. I was a bit nervous, though I managed to stay calm enough so that neither of us would break down.

The police officer stepped out of his car and walked towards us.

"Where are you off to?" he asked, removing his sunglasses. It distracted me for a bit. I don't really see people wear sunglasses at night that much.

"Just taking her home, officer," I said.

"Girlfriend?" he asked.

"No, sir, just a friend."

Elise continued to twiddle with her phone.

"License and registration please," he demanded in a calm voice. I opened my wallet and pulled out my license, shaking a bit. "I'm going to grab the registration from the glove compartment," I told the officer, just to make sure. Then I opened the glove compartment to get the car registration and handed it over to him.

"You look a little too young to drive," he said. I noticed another cop car stop behind us. Another police officer emerged, and he slowly made his way to Elise's side of the car.

"Thank you, officer," I said with a little comedy. But I was panicking inside. Not only would I be cited for drunk driving, but I had an intoxicated minor in the car with me as well. A lot of thoughts ran through my head. Scenarios of my possible future started popping up, and they weren't nice. I would surely fail the test if he asked me to take it. Heck, I could barely recite the alphabet when I'm sober. If I had to do it backwards in that condition, I would be royally screwed. The other cop was just talking to Elise about her cellphone, making conversation.

"You know what you did?" he asked. I really had no idea. I didn't know what I did wrong.

"I have no clue, sir," I said honestly.

"You ran a red light," he said, continuing to look at my license. Apparently, when I made a right turn on a red light, I didn't stop. I could have sworn it was still yellow when I turned. But I didn't want to aggravate him any further. He didn't seem to notice that we were drinking beforehand, and I wanted to keep it that way.

He wrote something down on a piece of paper and handed it to me. I felt like I was dumped. The amount was $445. Whew. That was a ton of money. But I was lucky that was the only thing he cited me for. It could have been worse, much worse. He gave me back my license and registration and patted the hood of my car.

"Drive safely," he said and walked back towards his car. The other cop walked away too.

"That was close. I thought we were going to jail for sure," I said.

"Jack, that was scary," said Elise. I could tell that she was relieved too.

A few minutes later, we left the scene, and I got her home safely.

Back in the present, I maneuvered through LA traffic and into the familiar side streets that led to her house. I was somehow able to memorize the way there, even though it had been quite a while since I had been to her house. We stopped right in front of her house. I helped her unload her luggage and walked her to the door.

She hugged me tightly. "Thank you," she said.

Just as I was about to walk away, I turned around and kissed her on the lips, but it was no more than a peck. "I'll see you around," I said. It seemed like I caught her off-guard, but it was a little awkward. She didn't really kiss me back, nor did she resist. She was even smiling slightly afterward.

"Yup, I'll see you soon," she said faintly.

I woke up to my lonely room the next day. No Elise, no one to say good morning to. I slowly rummaged through my old stash of letters, hidden under the bed in an old box. I found the ones Elise wrote to me back in high school and pulled them out. She used to call me "Cliffy," and I used to call her "Miffy". I always thought it was a bit childish but sweet in a way. After reading them, I somehow got the urge to go see her again. I grabbed my phone and texted her.

"Morning! You want to get some breakfast?" I asked.

"That would be nice. I'm hungry," she replied.

"I'll pick you up around eight. Wear something nice."

"Sure thing, mister," she said.

Without a second thought, I leaped into my car and drove towards her house.

Just as I exited the freeway, I received a text message. But I didn't get the chance to read it until I was near her house.

"Sorry, I can't today. Something came up," I read.

When I turned at the corner near her house, I realized why. I saw her crying in front of her door. Kneeling in front of her and carrying a bunch of flowers was a guy who was also crying. She was holding him closely.

I grabbed my phone and texted her one last time. "Goodbye, Miffy."

I watched as she took out her phone. After looking at it, she looked towards where I parked. Tears running down her brown eyes, the very same eyes that once took hold of me, finally let me go. I drove away broken but free, and I read the last text message I would get from her for a while.

"Goodbye, Cliffy."

OUR OWN CROSS TO CARRY

I wasn't sure if I was dreaming or if I was awake. I found myself wearing a white robe and barefoot. I was positive that I was in my bed, wearing pajamas with an image I'm too embarrassed to be caught in as an adolescent. I explored my surroundings, but there was nothing much to see except a long flight of stairs across from me, similar to the kind of stairs I imagined that rich people would have in their houses. It glittered and looked more expensive than marble. All of a sudden, I felt like I was gripping something. When I looked, there was a small wooden cross in my hand. "Where did that come from?" I asked myself. I couldn't figure it out, though it did feel like I had been carrying it for a long time.

Everything around me was white, as if I was photoshopped into a blank canvas. There was nowhere to go except the stairs. I made my way up the stairs slowly. The more I kept ascending, the more I could hear something. It was faint, but there was definitely a sound coming from somewhere. I kept looking around to see if there were other people besides myself, but I could see no one. I kept going higher and higher; I even ran for a little while, but somehow, I didn't feel tired. I looked ahead, and the stairs seemed like they had no end, though I finally saw other people or, at least, silhouettes of them. I was a little relieved that I wasn't alone on this endless staircase. They were, however, too far away to see or hear me from where I was. Didn't look like they were looking around either. They just kept going up the stairs.

I made my way up the seemingly infinite stairway faster in an attempt to catch up to them. Somehow, the cross I had on my hand grew a little bigger and heavier, but I could still bear it. After what seemed like hours, I felt relieved. This wasn't an endless staircase after all. I could finally see the end in sight. But there were suddenly a lot of clouds around me, which I found very strange. I tried pinching myself a couple of times to see if this was a dream, but nothing happened. I was still in this bizarre place.

After reaching the end of the stairs, I unexpectedly found myself in the back of a line. It was moving pretty quickly though. "Well, this beats the Theme Parks or the DMV" I thought to myself.

In front of me was a middle-aged man. He had a cross as well, but it was a lot bigger than the one I had. The others also had crosses on them. "Uh oh. Am I dead? Weird..." I told myself. "If this is where we go after death, it is a lot different than what I imagined, but there aren't any flames or evil monsters, so I guess I'm not in hell."

When I could no longer hold in my curiosity, I finally asked the man what the line was for; he said, "It's to get inside the kingdom. My family is waiting for me there," he said.

"Kingdom?" I asked again to clarify, but he ignored me and kept walking forward. At last, it was my turn. There was an old man sitting on a chair right outside a big golden arc. It reminded somehow of a certain popular fast food chain. "It couldn't be. There is no way they'd have a franchise here too," I mumbled.

"What are you doing here, young man?" he asked calmly and smiled. "Where is your ticket?"

"I don't know, sir. I went up the stairs, and here I am," I replied.

"I see. No ticket, eh?" said the old man "See that house over there?" He pointed to a rickety house on the side.

I was sure it wasn't there before, but there it was: a really big house on top of clouds. For some reason, I feel like I'd seen it before.

"Yes, it looks very familiar," I said.

"Indeed," said the old man, smiling. "Before I let you pass through these gates, I need you to go in that house and do some chores for the owner. If you do what they ask, I'll let you in. Sound good?"

I nodded and walked towards the house.

I knocked on the door a few times. An old lady opened it and told me to come inside. She was so warm and friendly that my body automatically stepped inside on its own. She led me to a dimly lit living room and motioned for me to sit down. I complied and instantly felt like a big weight was lifted off my shoulders. It felt so comfortable to sit down after being on my feet for a while.

"Would you like a glass of water?" she asked. I wasn't really thirsty, but I didn't want to offend her by saying no. "Yes," I answered. She went to the kitchen and came back with an empty glass and set it on a small table in front of me.

"Pardon me, ma'am, but the glass seems to be empty," I told her.

She smiled at me and told me to close my eyes for a minute.

I did as she told me, and everything went black.

When I opened my eyes, I found myself at another familiar place. I was at my old elementary school. I saw my younger self and some of my old friends, whose names I can't seem to remember, running about the place, but they couldn't see me. It was like I was invisible. I was probably around 8 years old at the time. I followed them closely as they sped up the stairways and made their way to the topmost floor of the building. I looked at them and immediately knew what was going to happen. I saw the younger version of myself reach for his pocket and take out a small rock. He suddenly dropped it to the first floor. My friends did the same. They immediately ran away as fast as they could without looking if they hit something or not. But I looked down. I saw a man massaging his swollen head. His glasses were broken, and there were a few drops of blood on the floor. I went downstairs to get a closer look. It was my third-grade teacher. He immediately made his way to the nurse's office. But it was empty. At the time, we didn't have a school nurse because of a funding issue. A nurse from another school stopped by on Tuesdays and Thursdays for a few hours, but it must have been an off day. Instead, he went to the principal and asked if he could take the day off because he couldn't see well and his head was hurting. But she refused him because there was no substitute teacher available that day. He seemed very distraught. I followed him to the classroom and watched him painfully trying to keep it together.

It all went by really fast, like everything was fast forwarded on a DVD player. He dismissed the kids immediately after the bell rang, then he grabbed his things and left the classroom slightly staggering. I continued to follow him down the stairs. It was painful to watch. He was grabbing on to the handrail and had some difficulty walking down the steps. I realized that he couldn't see very well because his glasses were broken. I tried to help him, but I couldn't touch him. I continued to follow him just to make sure he got home safely. He was finally off the school grounds; he reached the street and waited for a cab. But something was wrong. He continued to walk towards the road because he couldn't see where he was going. It happened in seconds.

There was a violent shrieking sound from a car brake, followed by a crashing sound, and I saw that my teacher was lying on the floor, covered with blood. The driver was in a hurry. He didn't even bother to stop. Crowds gathered around him, and they murmured to each other as they watched him.

Suddenly, it hit me. It was my fault that my teacher died that day. "I murdered someone?" I said to myself. Everything suddenly went black again.

I opened my eyes, and tears came rushing down. I found myself back in the house again with the old lady sitting across from me. She seemed to be knitting something. As I looked at her, I felt the cross in my hand get heavier.

"Dear boy, you mustn't blame yourself. Maybe it wasn't your rock that hit him," she said smiling.

She was right, but it didn't make me feel better. I was part of it. I threw the first rock.

The glass that stood in front of me was no longer empty. It was full of water all along.

I wiped away my tears, but I couldn't help feeling bad. I drank the water slowly, as if to drown away my guilt.

When I finished, the old lady was gone. Instead, there was an odd looking fellow with a thick mustache sitting where she sat. He seemed really happy to see me.

"I'm the owner of the house. Like everyone else, if you don't have a ticket, you have to do a small chore for me. Follow me so we can get started," he said enthusiastically. I walked behind him, and he led me to a giant garden. I felt like an ant compared to the size of it. The field of flowers seemed to stretch endlessly. There were different kinds of flowers; some of them were really beautiful. Some I've never seen before. But what stood out the most were a bunch of weeds in a small corner. They seemed ugly and looked like they didn't belong there among the beauty of what surrounded them.

"See those weeds over there?" he said, while pointing at them. "I need you to pluck them out one by one."

"Yes, sir," I said. I walked to the garden and knelt down; I felt the soft soil on my feet. In the real world, I wasn't really into gardening, nor did I care for plants much. But being barefoot on the soil, it felt like I was connected to everything. When I looked at the other plants around me, I started to feel disgust towards the weeds, and I was determined to remove them all. I started to pull on a tall weed that was sticking out, but it just wouldn't budge.

I looked around for the old man, but he was no longer there. I tried to pull it one more time, and images suddenly filled my head. I relived a bunch of memories that have been buried in my mind. I saw myself as a four-year-old boy pocketing a candy bar from a small department store without paying for it. Then, I was thirteen, yelling at my mom for accidentally unplugging my video game console while she was cleaning. Every moment I was unkind to others, every time I cheated, everything I felt bad for, and every time I did wrong, it all came back to me. More and more weeds started to pop out in the garden. I was able to pull them out, but there were so many of them. It must have taken me days to finish, but I finally pulled the last one out. When I was finished, the cross I carried grew even bigger. I had to lift it on my shoulder in order to move it. I don't know why I was compelled to carry it, but somehow it felt like it was attached to me, like it was a part of me, it was me. The house and the garden disappeared from my sight, and I found myself in front of the gate again. There were more people than the last time. But I needed to go in there. Not sure why, but I felt like that's where I should go. I fell in line again, the cross gradually gaining more weight as I got closer to the door. I didn't think I would get tired here, but when I finally reached the gate again, I was panting.

"Ah, it's you again. We've been waiting for you," said the old man. "Come in, come in! The owner said that you are good to go."

Somehow, I was glad. It felt really good to be inside. When I set foot inside the gate, I saw more people carrying crosses than there were outside. Some looked heavier than mine, and some looked really light. "Go up that hill. Everyone needs to go there," said the old man from behind the gate.

I looked up at the hill. It was quite far. I started having doubts whether I would make it or not as the cross grew heavier still.

People were stumbling and falling from the weight of the cross that they carried. I, too, suffered the same fate. It was a tough climb, and I couldn't even reach the middle part of the hill. The cross was too heavy for me.

I fell down several times. I just couldn't get up there. A friendly looking, middle-aged man with a white robe appeared before me. He looked at me with kind eyes. He was smiling at me. He seemed like someone I'd known my whole life, but I knew I'd never met him.

"Do you need help with that, young man?" he asked.

"Yes, please, if you don't mind. I think this might be a two-man carry situation, like those boxes in an office that they tell you not to carry alone," I said jokingly.

He just smiled and grabbed my cross. It suddenly disappeared.

"What happened to it?" I asked.

"Don't worry. I took care of it," he said, still smiling.

I looked at him more closely. He was trying to hide it, but I could tell that he seemed really tired.

"Are you okay, sir?" I asked him.

"Oh. I'll be alright. Just remember that you're not alone and that I'll always have your back," he said. I studied him more carefully. I had not seen it at first. I closed my eyes and opened them again just to make sure it was real.

Uncontrollable tears ran down my face. I fell on the ground from what I saw.

On his back was a giant cross. Taller than any building I've ever seen. I couldn't see the end of it.

I came back to my room. My eyes were still full of tears, and my knees were shaking.

At that moment, I made a vow to live my life as best as I could and as kindly as I could, so when I pass through those gates again, he will not have to carry my cross for me.

LOVE ON A
TWO-WAY STREET

He couldn't believe it was her when he saw her. As he pulled up to the car, a rush of anxiety overtook him. He hurried to stop and get out of the tow truck, his heart pounding as he met her out on the side of the road.

Her eyes were huge under the moonlight, though she looked like she had been crying. Disbelief was written all over her face.

"Candice." All he could speak was her name. His voice came out quivering.

"Harry," she responded quietly, not knowing what else to say. "What are you doing here?"

"Towing your car, apparently." Harry smiled at her, trying to lighten her up, but her facial expression didn't change. He could feel her watching him as he moved her car up onto the truck.

"How are you?" Harry hadn't realized Candice had come up tentatively next to him in an attempt to make conversation. "How have you been?"

"Alright," he responded. "You?"

"Alright." She was quiet for a moment, and Harry didn't want to stop talking to her quite yet. Next to them, cars zipped by, their lights blurring into each other underneath the dark sky.

"I thought you were in the military."

"I was."

"What happened?"

"Hey, can I give you a ride back home?" Harry sighed, not wanting to go through the details of his military days. He felt guilty at the hurt that flushed her cheeks.

"If it's no trouble, yes, please."

"Of course, it's not." Harry rushed to open the passenger's side door for Candice, and she got in, nearly tripping on the way up. Before Harry could stop himself, he let out a small laugh, remembering how clumsy Candice always was. He felt a little better when Candice looked back at him and giggled.

Candice felt like she was supposed to be embarrassed, but she realized that he had always known that she didn't have the best coordination.

Harry returned to the driver's side and jumped in. "Where do you live?"

"Creepy much?" The playful tone in her voice brought Harry back to their high school days. He'd found himself missing her sing often during his deployment. Now, hearing them made him feel good somehow.

Candice also had a singe of nostalgia. She hadn't acted that way in while.

"Hey now," he said laughing. He took off down the road. "Do you still like country?"

"Of course! You thought I'd grow out of that?"

"I prayed you'd grow out of that," he said gingerly.

Candice hit Harry playfully, but he changed the radio anyways to her favorite country radio station.

"Aw, you remembered!" There was a twinkle in her eye when Harry looked over at her.

"You thought I wouldn't? We played this station constantly because you loved it so much."

"You loved it, too!"

"That's a total exaggeration." Harry shook his head. "I was okay with it because you loved it. And I loved you."

Candice went quiet after hearing that; she remembered the relationship they had a few years ago and that it had ended on a sour note. Harry realized what he said. It came out so easily, as though it was meant to reach Candice's ears, and for the millionth time that night, he thought about the long days he had spent just lying in bed with Candice and watching her wake up. It had always been the fondest moments of his life.

"It's the house right there," Candice said as Harry turned onto her street. "If you could just park the car for me in the driveway, that would be great."

For some reason, she just wanted to get out as fast as she could. Mixed emotions and memories suddenly swelled up inside her, and she felt like she needed to be alone. But at the same time, she also wanted to be with him. She missed him.

"Of course." He came to a stop and got out to unload the truck.

"How much do I owe you?" Candice asked as she followed him outside.

"It's on the house." Harry flashed a quick smile.

"Are you sure? Won't your boss be angry at you?"

"I'll tell him I did it for an old friend."

"Alright, well, let me at least make us dinner then. I loved catching up with you in the car, and I don't want it to end just yet."

Right after she said it, she immediately regretted it. It was as if she wasn't in control of herself and she said it automatically.

"That would be really great," he said. Harry was also a little hungry, and he always loved her cooking. Something he hadn't had in a long while.

She smiled and led the way. When she took his hand and pulled him along, it was like his fingers laced perfectly with hers. She seemed to realize what she had done, and she pulled her hand back, looking at him with red on her cheeks.

After she grabbed his hand, he immediately wanted to stop her. But he couldn't for some reason. This was wrong, and he knew it. He already felt guilty about how he left things with her. Aside from that, he hadn't had the guts to tell her that he is getting married soon.

We're just old friends catching up! He thought to himself.

Candice unlocked the door, and as soon as they walked inside, a little dog rushed up to greet them.

"That's Ivy," she told Harry, leaning down to pet the schnauzer. It jumped at her legs before running up to sniff Harry.

"You always wanted a dog."

"Now, I finally have one." When Harry looked at Candice, she was gazing down fondly at Ivy.

"It gets lonely sometimes in here."

Her eyes held deep meaning in them, and Harry tried to ignore it. "So, what's for dinner?"

"Leftover pizza?" Candice winced as she suggested it. "I'm sorry. I've been so busy at work- "

"No, our pizza dates were always our favorites," Harry cut her off.

"Okay, I'll be right back." She rushed to the kitchen to heat some up while Harry sat down in the dining room. The apartment looked exactly as he would've imagined. The walls were a soft white color, and paintings were strung along them. Her front room was filled with a cozy couch and chairs in front of a small tv, and the dining room was just big enough for the table.

Moments later, Candice rushed back in with plates and Dominos pizza. She handed him a few slices.

"You can never go wrong with Dominos," he told her, taking a couple slices. All Candice did was nod her head as she took hers and started eating.

It was silent for a while, but Harry didn't mind. He enjoyed Candice's company and could've sat there forever.

"Why did you leave me?" She suddenly blurted, pain playing across her face. Her lips quivered the slightest bit. Harry clutched his chest.

"It wasn't because I didn't love you," he said quietly. "I thought the military was the only way I could make something of myself."

"I was so broken for months after. I loved you with everything I had." She stared at her plate, trying not to cry.

"Do you still?" Harry knitted his eyebrows as his stomach spun inside him. He wasn't sure he wanted to know the answer.

"I do." She said it so quietly that it could've been his imagination if he hadn't watched her lips. She got up and came around to his side of the table, her eyes staring deep into his. "I never stopped."

He let her move closer until she was sitting in his lap. Her slim hands were trembling as they traced his face, outlining his cheeks. He couldn't look away, and finally, he kissed her.

It was so familiar that it felt like yesterday was the last time they had been together. He fell into her, shutting his eyes so tight that he hoped he would never come out. He kissed her with the passion he hadn't been able to give for the last four years, hoping she could read the apology in his hands roaming her body, his lips, his tongue.

Harry picked her up. Slowly stumbling blindly up the stairs, they found their way to her room, their intimacy unbroken. He laid her on the bed and kissed her neck, in the one sweet spot she'd always loved. Both of them were consumed with a bliss that made it impossible to stop. Harry couldn't resist what he shouldn't have done. What they both had done.

The next few days were the best Harry had ever had. He was at Candice's house every chance they got, and almost every time, he was supposed to regret it. But somehow it felt right. He just needed a chance to tell Candice. He just couldn't bring himself to do it. But he knew it wouldn't last the first morning Candice brought up a relationship. Not unless he made a decision that would forsake another.

"What if we try this again?" she said, basking in the morning light. The light decorated her body so perfectly, it was like the sun was meant for her.

"What if we get into a relationship, and this time, it lasts?"

"I don't know." Harry sat up so fast, Candice couldn't help but think that something was wrong.

"What is it?"

"No, it's nothing." He shook his head and got up to get dressed. "I have work, though. Do you need a ride or anything?"

"No, I don't work until later." Through her smile, Harry could see the hurt, but he didn't wait to give himself a chance to bring it to the surface.

"Okay. I'll see you later, then." He walked out without another word, grabbing everything he needed. Getting in his car, he made his way to the towing company. As if to give him enough time to be away from Candice, his phone rang. Tabatha was calling.

"Hey," he said as casually as ever.

"Hi, my love. Did you start the guest list?" Her voice sounded heavy.

"No, I completely forgot!" Harry shut his eyes and nearly let out a groan. "I'll do it today. I promise."

"Okay. I know the wedding isn't for a few months, but I want everything to be perfect when I marry you. That's alright, isn't it?"

"Of course, it is. I want it to be perfect, too." He wasn't so sure his words were true.

"Okay. I hope work goes well, and I'll see you when you get home. I'm sorry you were working all night."

"Thanks, babe. I gotta go."

"Bye, I love you." Harry hung up, hoping it looked more like he'd accidentally cut her off than he'd just refused to say it back.

He'd met Tabatha when he joined the army a few years ago. At first, they were just good friends working together. But as time went by, working in close proximity with each other, the two just got on naturally, and they'd stuck by each other ever since.

Their friendship evolved one day; he remembered the day she walked into his room in tears. Without saying anything, she lifted up her shirt, showing Harry the bruises that scored the entire front and back of her body.

"Who did this?!" he asked, fury boiling in his throat. But she wouldn't say who it was.

"Tabatha, you have to tell me. This isn't right," he said. Finally, she revealed that, over the years, she had been blackmailed by their company commander. He somehow got a hold of a picture of her naked with an officer from another company. If it got out, both her and the officer would be in big trouble. Threatening to release it, she had been abused by him physically and sexually.

The next time the company gathered, Harry walked up to their commander and punched him so hard, he was knocked to the ground. "How does it feel?" he yelled as he kicked him in the stomach brutally. "Do you like it?"

"Hey, break it up!" Soldiers had run up and distanced the two from each other.

"You've been abusing her this entire time!" Harry boomed so that all the other soldiers heard. "You don't belong here!"

A few days later, Harry was booted out of the Army. He was lucky he didn't have to go through a court martial. After the military gathered evidence on their commander, he was immediately court marshalled and sent to prison. After being abused for so long, Tabatha was finally free, and she had Harry to thank for that. Yet, she couldn't help but feel responsible for Harry ending his military career so abruptly.

"Don't feel bad," he used to say. "I'm glad I got out of an organization that lets people like that wear a uniform and allows them to move up in the ranks."

Tabatha slowly fell in love with him over the course of a few months, and Harry too had thought he'd fallen in love with her when he'd proposed, but now, he wasn't so sure.

All day, all he could think about was Candice and the way it felt to be with her. By the end of the day, he knew that he had to decide between the two.

In his mind, he tossed a coin as he sat up from his desk. He was going to let fate decide. Right after work, if he got to Candice's and she was home, he would confess everything to her and leave Tabatha for Candice. It hurt him to think about the look on Tabatha's face when he told her what had happened.

If Candice wasn't home, he would find a way to break to her gently later on and continue as if he and Candice had never been. He knew this was wrong, and it broke him inside. But he needed to choose. It was time.

He realized that he forgot to charge his phone while at work, but he had already made up his mind and immediately drove off towards where Candice lived.

Pulling up to Candice's house with his heart beating loudly in his chest, he drove up into her driveway, praying at the same time to let her be home. He knew that her car wasn't there because it was at the repair shop. He got out, taking his time, and made his way up to the door. He knew that the doorbell was broken after being there a couple of times, so he knocked loudly, so she'd hear him if she was home.

Harry must've waited for at least ten minutes, hoping Candice would answer the door. He knocked every so often, but by the time he left, it was clear she wasn't there. His heart felt shattered despite the future he knew he had waiting for him with Tabatha.

Tears pooled in his eyes as he got in his car and drove back home, selfishly hoping Tabatha would be there. He completely missed the little yellow jeep that Candice was driving, turning the corner less than a block away. As he drove away, Candice caught a glimpse of him and called his phone. But it was off.

All of a sudden, Candice had a feeling that she needed to see him and talk to him right then and there. He was already some distance away from her, but she could still catch up. Instead of parking, she decided to go after him. After a few minutes, she could finally see his car again. He wasn't driving too fast, but she knew, if he got on the highway, she might lose him. Her car didn't do too well at higher speeds anymore. She thought she still had some time, but she realized he was already turning towards the freeway entrance. There weren't too many cars. The highway felt abandoned, lonely even.

"I can make it!" she said to herself. She was close. Just a little more.

But her hope faded when she heard a familiar sound. Her car had sputtered a few times. She knew she had to stop on the shoulder or she would be in trouble. Seconds away and she would have caught up. But it was too late. The car had given up. She had given up. Harry was gone.

THE BOUCHARDS
Sleeping Child

Chris Bouchard peered over the book in his hands. The 8:20 train to Marseilles began like any other train ride Chris had taken in the past. But something was different about this one. This time, he saw – her. She was gorgeous; her chestnut hair fell in soft curls around her shoulders. Her skin was smooth, with a slight flush to her cheeks and a natural pink tint to her lips. Her delicate eyes were a deep green. Chris knew this because they had wandered over to him seven times already (not that he was counting). Now, on the eighth time, her eyes met and locked with his.

Chris sucked in his breath but tried to keep his face calm. A slight smile played across her lips, and those dazzling green eyes twinkled, almost undoing Chris completely. He gave a nervous chuckle and began to stand up when, suddenly, the train screeched to a halt. All the lights flickered then went out completely. An announcement came over the PA system that the power had gone out. They also mentioned not to worry and that it would be resolved quickly.

Chris looked back to the lovely woman sitting a few rows behind him, and she giggled. She smiled at him and gave him an inviting gaze – his move.

He gave her a boyish grin and made his way over, plopping down in the seat right next to her.

"Hi," Chris said breathlessly.

"Hello there." The enchanting woman smiled and shyly tucked a strand of smooth hair behind her ear.

"Do you like books?" he asked her, holding out the one in his hand: *The Shining* by Stephen King.

"Hmm, I do like interesting books like this one." She shot him a coy grin. "But I also like interesting men who read interesting books."

Chris almost fell out of his seat. "My name is Chris. Chris Bouchard," he said quickly. He held out his hand, swallowing hard.

"Marlene," she said, shaking his hand with another giggle. "I'm Marlene. So, what do you do for a living, Chris? Are you a writer? A librarian? A professor?"

Chris chuckled. "I'm a singer," he told her. "I mostly play in jazz clubs around Marseille. What about you?"

"I'm an actress," Marlene smiled. "Well, an aspiring actress. I'm a café barista during the day."

"Ah, a lady after my heart." Chris pretended to clutch his chest. "The arts and caffeine, my two greatest vices."

Marlene laughed at his antics. It was the sweetest sound that Chris had ever heard. "Well," she said, "maybe you should swing by my café sometime. I would be happy to help with the caffeine vice."

"I would love that." Chris's eyes lit up.

"Great." Marlene gave him a soft smile. "Café Noisette, 3 pm tomorrow."

The train's lights came back on, and it began to roll slowly forward again.

Chris looked deep into Marlene's eyes. "I'll be there."

***

Years passed, and Marlene and Chris fell more madly in love with each passing one. They met for coffee as often as their schedules – and their limited budgets – allowed. They began writing letters to each other, passing them back and forth each time they met. They dreamed of their futures, recounted stories of their pasts, and reveled in their present – the beautiful actress and the rugged singer – a match made in heaven.

They quickly moved in together, just outside of Marseilles, France. It was a small apartment, barely big enough for two people, but it was their home. Even then, they continued to pass letters and little notes back and forth, leaving them all over the apartment for the other to find.

One day, five years to the day they met, Marlene handed Chris a letter as he sat eating breakfast. The paper had a wax seal binding it together and was lightly scented with her favorite perfume. Chris chuckled as she handed it to him, shaking his head.

"What's this, love?" he asked with a smile. "This is a bit much, don't you think?"

Marlene giggled and swatted his arm playfully. "Oh, just open it! It's a special occasion."

Chris carefully opened the seal and delicately unfolded the paper. As his eyes moved across the page, he smiled. Then he laughed out loud. Then his eyes began to mist over. Finally, he slapped the letter down on the table and jumped out of his seat.

"You're kidding!" he cried out.

Marlene laughed, with a few tears trickling down her cheeks. "I'm not kidding, sweetheart. Not in the slightest."

Chris practically jumped across the table to scoop her up in his arms. He planted a tender kiss on Marlene's lips as his own tears threatened to spill over. He cupped her face in his hands and whispered hoarsely, "I love you, Marlene. I love you so much. And I promise, I'm going to take such good care of you – and our baby."

Marlene cried softly as she clung to Chris with one hand and rested the other hand on her pregnant belly. "I love you too, Chris. And I have no doubt you'll be the best father the world has ever seen."

* * *

Eight months later, Chris burst into Marseille's women's hospital, panting and pouring sweat from his forehead. He rushed to the information desk.

"Hello, yes, I'm looking for Marlene Bouchard! She's my wife, and she paged me while I was at work, and she's having our baby, it's a boy, and –"

"Room 207, sir." The woman at the information desk practically rolled her eyes as she spoke in a dull tone.

"Oh...thank you!" Chris called over his shoulder as he fled down the hall.

He sprinted through the maternity ward, frantically dodging wheelchairs and doctors, and scanning the room numbers. *Room 203, 205 – ah! Room 207!* Chris breathed a sigh of relief as he rushed into the room.

Marlene was lying on the hospital bed, surrounded by nurses and doctors. Her eyes were squeezed shut, her teeth were gritted, and her fingers were white from gripping the bed's handlebars. A contraction seized her body, and she cried out in pain. Chris ran to her side and grabbed her hand, kissing her forehead despite the sheen of sweat that glistened on her skin.

"Oh, Chris!" Marlene gasped. Her face was pale, and her eyes rolled back in her head.

"It's okay. It's okay, baby. I got here as quickly as I could. I'm here. Breathe, breathe...you're doing great, Marlene." Chris stroked her hair and helped Marlene brace for another contraction.

One doctor came to Chris's side. "You're her husband, sir?" she asked.

Chris nodded. "Yes, I'm Chris Bouchard. I'm her husband."

The doctor nodded. "I'm Dr. Lafayette, Head Obstetrician. Nice to meet you." Dr. Lafayette straightened her shoulders then continued.

"Mr. Bouchard, your wife has been fighting bravely, but I'm afraid there have been some complications. We have a decision to make here."

"Wh-what do you mean? I know she's delivering a few weeks early, but what exactly do you mean complications?" Chris sputtered.

The doctor shook her head. "I'm afraid both your wife's vitals and the baby's vitals are plummeting quickly. We need to go into emergency surgery, stat, but we need to know which one to prioritize."

"Prioritize?" Chris stepped back, and his stomach twisted into a thousand knots. His heart leaped into his throat, and his vision began to blur.

Dr. Lafayette placed a hand on his shoulder. "I know this is difficult, Mr. Bouchard, but we have to know."

"Yes, of course. Marlene...please don't let anything happen to Marlene."

"No, Chris." Marlene moaned from her position on the bed. She gripped his hand tightly with both of hers. "I'll be fine. I promise. This baby deserves a chance. Please, Chris, we need to give our baby a chance."

Chris hesitated and shook his head at a loss for words.

Marlene gripped his hand even tighter. "Trust me, Chris. Trust me. We will both be alright." She offered a weak smile through a grimace of pain.

Chris began to see stars. He couldn't believe the choice before him.

"Mr. Bouchard," Dr. Lafayette pressed.

Chris managed to nod his head. "Okay...okay, yes. The baby is the priority."

The doctor nodded and motioned to her team of nurses. They began to wheel Marlene out the door to the OR. Chris ran alongside them as they went, desperately clinging to Marlene's hand.

"Marlene," he said as tears began to leak from his eyes. "Marlene, I love you. I love you dearly, and I'll be right here waiting for you."

Marlene's eyes were closed, but she smiled faintly. "I...I love you...I love you, Chris," she mumbled.

Chris released her hand as they reached the doors to the operating wing. He watched helplessly as the nurses hastily wheeled Marlene down the hall, disappearing around the corner. He took a shaking breath and finally let his tears fall freely.

* * *

Hours later, Dr. Lafayette emerged from the same double-doors she had taken Marlene through. She held a little bundle of blankets in her arms.

Chris jumped up as soon as he saw her and ran over. "Well?" he said breathlessly. "How is she, Doctor? How are they?"

Dr. Lafayette smiled grimly and handed him the bundle in her arms, which began to fuss! Chris pulled back one of the blankets to reveal the most perfect baby he had ever seen. He let out a single laugh and held his baby boy close to his chest, sniffling through his smile.

"How is Marlene?" he asked.

Dr. Lafayette sighed heavily. "Mr. Bouchard, I'm very sorry. We did everything we could, but...Marlene didn't make it. She's gone, sir."

THE BOUCHARDS
The Actor

Twenty Years Later

Chris sighed and tossed the morning paper back onto the kitchen table. He took a long sip of coffee as he stared out the window at the Quebec mountains rising in the distance.

"More coffee, honey?" his girlfriend, Rita, stood from across the table and went to the coffee pot. Chris had known Rita for a few years, but they had only recently gotten together as a couple. She had moved in a few months ago, and things were going well – as well as Chris could hope for, anyway.

After Marlene's passing, Chris moved from France to Quebec, Canada, to be closer to his sister. He didn't know the first thing about raising a child, so he needed all the help he could get. His son, Michael, was the spitting image of his mother. So, though Chris loved his son dearly, just looking at him sometimes made Chris sad.

As if on cue, Mike shuffled into the kitchen, rubbing his eyes and yawning. His 20-year-old frame was lean, and his chestnut brown hair was slightly curly at the ends. His emerald green eyes seemed to look right through your soul, much like his mother's had.

"Good morning," Mike mumbled as he sat down next to Chris.

Chris nodded at his son and handed him a mug for coffee with a smile.

"Good morning, Mike!" Rita said cheerfully. "How did your audition go last night?"

Just like his mother, Mike had fallen in love with acting. He was struggling to make a name for himself here in Quebec, but God bless him, did he ever try.

Mike shrugged as Rita poured coffee into his mug. "It went okay, I suppose. Typical 'we'll call you' response. Actually, Dad, I was hoping to talk to you about that today." Mike looked expectantly at his father.

Rita set the pot of coffee down. "Well, I'll just leave you two to it, then," she said with a smile. She patted Mike on the arm and kissed the top of Chris's head before leaving the kitchen.

Mike cleared his throat, suddenly becoming nervous. "Um, Dad? You know I've been trying this acting thing for a while. It's my passion; it's what I want to do for the rest of my life."

Chris nodded as he peered at his son from over the top of his reading glasses. Mike looked positively green. The kid was so nervous.

Mike cleared his throat before continuing. "But the scene is kind of dry here in Quebec, so I was thinking – wondering, really, if you...if you would support me if I moved to Hollywood?"

Chris stared at Mike unblinking. A heavy cocktail of emotions began to swirl around inside his stomach. He was so proud of his son for pursuing his dream, yet was so scared to let his boy move away. He was thrilled that Mike's passions were the same as Marlene's, but his heart ached at the thought of the relationship those two could have shared.

Chris took a steadying breath and blinked the tears from his eyes. Mike took this as a terrible sign and began to backpedal.

"You know what, Dad? Never mind, it's stupid. I just have to keep trying harder here, that's all. Moving is a terrible idea; guess I was just waking up still. I can just –"

"You're going," Chris said.

Mike stopped and stared at him, hardly daring to breathe. "What did you say?"

"You're going," Chris repeated with a smile. "You're going to move to Hollywood and become a star. You're going to achieve your goals. I'm going to support you, and that includes helping to pay for moving costs. And when you've made it big, and your dear old Dad is ready for retirement, you're going to set him up with a mansion in the Hills and a '69 Corvette."

Mike's face slowly broke into a smile as his dad spoke. He launched himself from his chair and flung his arms around his father's shoulders, laughing in disbelief. He pulled back, his cheeks flushed with excitement.

"Thank you, Dad," he breathed. "Thank you so much."

"There's no need to thank me, son," Chris said with a laugh. "Your mother died giving you a chance to live a full life. You've got to take all the chances you can get."

"Well, I won't let you down. I promise. Before you know it, I'll be a celebrity!" Mike beamed.

* * *

Six months later, Mike toddled out of the front door of his apartment. His bathrobe had more than a few holes, but he couldn't afford a new one. Not yet, anyway. The compensation for playing extras in movies and TV shows was just enough to get by – but that was about it. He wasn't exactly living the celebrity life here in Hollywood.

Mike bent down to grab the newspaper on his doorstep with a groan. He straightened up, yawning and scratching his belly. He tugged at his overgrown hair and ran his hand over the two-day stubble on his face. He turned to go back into his apartment when he caught sight of his neighbor down the hall. The neighbor was shaking his head, staring at Mike – judging him.

Mike glared back then scowled as he hurried back inside and slammed the door behind him. He didn't need anyone else to remind him how pathetic he looked; he felt it in his very bones. Sighing, Mike opened his phone to check his bank account balance.

He winced. Not good.

Well, time to cast a wider net, he thought to himself. He opened the paper and shuffled through until he found the classifieds. He paused, steeling himself for the things to come (this was LA, after all), and began to read.

Wanted: dog therapist specializing in human-canine behavioral intervention.

Mike shook his head. No way.

In search of dancers to perform at my high-quality gentleman's club. The money be fallin' as long as you ballin'.

Mike twisted his face into a look of disgust and turned to the next page with a shudder.

Artist in need of a male model. No nudity, no funny business – keep your pants on. I just need a new someone to paint.

Mike nodded, staring out the tiny window of his apartment. *That doesn't sound half-bad,* he thought to himself. He tapped his chin as he looked at the hourly rate for the gig.

Without another thought, he snatched up his phone again and dialed the number listed on the ad.

"Hello? Yeah, hi, I saw your ad in the paper for a male painting model? Mike, my name is Mike Bouchard."

THE BOUCHARDS
Paint My Love

"Hi, you must be Mike! I'm Kristin. Kristen Lambert."

Mike almost dropped the half-eaten sandwich in his hand. The woman who had answered the door was the most beautiful woman he had ever seen – and he lived in California.

Kristin held out her hand with a smile. She had screaming blue eyes that pierced his heart. Her reddish-blonde hair was piled into a bun that sat on top of her head, but a few wild strands had managed to pull themselves loose, framing her freckled skin perfectly.

"Oh, um...hi. Yeah, I'm Mike. It's nice to meet you, Kristen." Mike started to take her outstretched hand but realized that he was still clinging to his sandwich. He awkwardly tried to shake Kristin's right hand with his left. *Wow. Smooth move, buddy,* he chided himself.

Kristin laughed. Not an oh-my-God-you're-so-stupid laugh, but a genuine, amused laugh.

"I like your priorities," she teased. "Come on in. My studio is also my living room, so feel free to make yourself at home."

A few hours later, Kristin stepped back from the canvas with a happy sigh. "Alright. Finished."

"Already?" Mike asked, flabbergasted. He stood up from the quirky armchair where he was posing reading the back of an album cover.

Kristin nodded enthusiastically. "Yep! Can you believe it? I've never painted this quickly before. It just felt so...natural. You made it so easy. You helped me feel like a true artist." She smiled shyly at him.

Mike's heart did a million flips in his chest.

"Well," he stepped closer to her, "maybe I'll have to come over here more often then. You know, to help you with your paintings."

Kristin also took a step closer to Mike. "Yeah," she said softly. "I would like that a lot."

Mike leaned down and gently pressed his lips to hers.

As the two of them fell to the ground, the painting of Mike fell off of Kristin's easel, leaving a giant smudge of paint on the white tile floor.

* * *

The next few weeks were almost as much of a blur as the following few years. Mike moved in with Kristin a month after their first encounter. They spent every waking minute together, helping each other find gigs and auditions. Their relationship was a spark that quickly grew into a burning flame.

But all flames must eventually burn down to a smolder.

The first two years were fantastic, as far as Mike was concerned. They were perfectly happy living as the starving artist couple, just scraping by every month. Then, the reality of life hit Kristen, and she decided to take a steady job at a local museum while continuing to paint on the side. Mike pressed on with his acting career, determined to be the next big thing in Hollywood. After countless roles as an extra, he finally landed his big break – the lead role in a shampoo commercial.

The appearance did make him quite a bit of money, but it was not the "big break" they had both thought it would be. Mike's agent stopped calling him within months of the commercial going off-air. Offers would come through for a role as an extra, but Mike would refuse. He claimed that those days were behind him, that it would look bad if he took those kinds of roles again. So, he slowly found himself without work. He would spend his days lying on the couch and staring at the television – aimlessly watching E! News and scrolling through the want ads on Craigslist.

Kristin felt sorry for him at first. Then she felt frustrated. Then, two weeks before their three-year anniversary, she felt *pissed*.

She had just gotten home from working a 12-hour shift at the museum. She slumped against the front door and kicked her shoes off with a sigh. Her feet ached so badly, all she wanted was to prop them up on the couch with a glass of wine in her hand. She gingerly stepped further into the apartment and rolled her eyes when she heard E! News coming from the TV.

As she walked through the kitchen, she saw the sink piled high with dirty dishes, even though she had asked Mike to take care of them – again. Kristin inwardly groaned but decided to let that one go. She made her way to the fridge and pulled out the bottle of her favorite wine. She paused and swirled the bottle in her hand.

Empty.

Freaking really? She thought. She grabbed a beer instead and began walking toward the living room. At least she could still relax and put her feet up. But as she passed the hallway leading to the bedroom, something caught her eye.

A giant pile of laundry was strewn across the floor, not sorted but not gathered into a mound, either – just thrown everywhere.

That was the breaking point.

Kristin slammed the bottle on the kitchen counter and marched into the living room, eyes flashing. She startled Mike, who was lying on the couch, playing on his phone and half-listening to the television. Kristin grabbed the remote from the cushion beside him and turned the TV off before throwing it against the wall so hard the batteries popped out.

"Whoa! What the hell, Kristin?" Mike sat up, somewhat angry but mostly confused.

"What the hell, me? What the hell back at you, Mike! What have you been doing all day?"

"I...well, um...I was working on..." Mike sputtered.

"Augh!" Kristin screamed as she buried her face in her hands. "Mike, I can't keep doing this! I've been at work all day, and you haven't done a single damn thing around the house! Look at the kitchen! Do you see the kitchen? And what the actual fuck happened with the laundry on the bedroom?"

"Oh, I was looking for my lucky shirt," Mike replied.

"You got an audition?"

Mike laughed. "No! No, I didn't get an audition; I'm holding out for the right one, but they keep sending me all these insignificant extra gigs. I'm not about that life anymore; it's not my passion."

Kristin stared at him so hard he thought he was going to melt. "Listen here, you man-child," she hissed. "I support us financially. I do the cooking, the cleaning, the laundry, and literally everything else for you. On the other hand, you sit here on the couch all day, picking your nose and wishing you were Tom Cruise."

Mike snorted. "I have never in my life wished that I was –"

"Shut up!" Kristin screamed. "Shut up, shut up, Mike! You're not listening to me! I'm exhausted! I need a break so fucking badly, and you refuse to help me take one! I need a break, Mike!"

Mike stood and got in her face. "You need a break? What about me, huh? I've been chasing my dreams for the last three years, but I haven't gotten the big one yet! Not even close! Maybe I need a break from your constant nagging and whining about how your life is so hard!"

"I was hoping for a proposal by now, Mike! Did you ever think of that? That maybe the girl who loves you would want to hear it just a little bit, that she would want some sort of commitment?"

"I can't propose, and you know it!" Mike thundered. "And even if I did have the money, I would have taken the ring back based on how you're acting right now!"

"GET OUT!" Kristin screamed.

Mike paused. "What? What did you say?"

"I said, get out, Mike! I can't stand to look at you for one second longer! You are such a lost little boy, and I can't spend my life being the mother you never had!" Hot, angry tears started to pour down Kristin's face.

Mike felt like she had just punched him in the face. "You don't mean that," he said softly.

"I do mean it! Oh my God, Mike, just get your crap and get the hell out of my life!" Kristin stormed to the balcony and slammed the door shut behind her, leaving Mike standing in the living room, stunned and hurt.

* * *

Mike took another long drag of the beer in front of him, polishing it off. The bartender came over and leaned against the counter.

"Another one, Mikey?" he asked.

"Sure, Carl. Thanks," Mike replied as he pinched his nose between his thumb and forefinger.

As Carl began to pour another round for Mike, a man came up and hopped up on the stool next to him.

"Hey! You're that guy from the shampoo commercial!" he said to Mike.

Mike nodded without looking up. "Yep, that was me," he mumbled. "And no, I don't do autographs."

The man laughed heartily. "Oh, I'm not here for any autographs, son! The name's Page, Stanley Page. I'm a manager and agent in this little ole town. Say, are you open to new roles at the moment?"

"That depends," Mike said with a belch. "What kind of roles are we talking about?"

Stanley Page laughed again. "Well, at the moment, I'm scouting for a superhero's sidekick. I'm working on the new Nebula Comics live-action film."

Mike perked up at this news and finally turned to face Stanley. "You're kidding."

Stanley shook his head with a grin. "No, I'm really not. So – are you interested?"

THE BOUCHARDS
25 Minutes

Mike walked down the street with a bounce in his step. It had been almost a year since Kristin kicked him out and he met his new manager at the bar. Since then, he had co-starred in two action movies and would begin work on a third in the coming weeks. His luck had sure turned around since that fateful night.

Of course, he thought about Kristin almost every day. He felt terrible for the way he acted that night and many nights before that, but he just couldn't bring himself to reach out. He wanted to get his life on track and in order before he could even consider asking Kristin to take him back.

Fortunately, that standard was quickly coming to fruition. With the income from the last couple of movies, Mike had managed to pay off his debts, get a bigger (and much nicer) apartment of his own, and even set some money aside. After this upcoming movie finished filming, he would have enough to buy Kristin the biggest rock she could find in LA.

Take every chance you can. Mike repeated his father's words to himself. He thought of his dad a lot more these days – Chris Bouchard was the greatest father anyone could ask for. He had supported Mike through his tough breakup and attended both premieres of Mike's movies, beaming with pride the whole time.

Mike smiled as he thought of how his father's eyes would twinkle if he told his dad that Kristin agreed to marry him. He practically skipped his way into the coffee shop, his favorite place to visit on Saturday afternoons. When he reached the counter, he stopped with surprise.

"Oh my God! Lena!"

Lena was a mutual friend of Mike's and Kristin's, but he hadn't seen her in months. Kristin "got to keep her" when they separated, so Mike had kept his distance. But now, she was standing in front of him, working at his favorite coffee shop in town.

Lena smiled at him. "Hey, Mike! How are you doing?"

"Good, good! I finally broke my way onto the set of a couple of movies," he said with a grin.

Lena laughed. "Yeah, I saw that! Congratulations, that's awesome."

"Thanks," Mike looked at his toes then back at Lena. "How is, um... how is Kristin?"

Lena's eyes got wide, and she cleared her throat. "She's...she's fine. What drink are you getting today?"

Mike chuckled nervously. "An americano, please. Lena, is everything alright? Is Kristin okay?"

"Yeah! Yep, she's doing just fine!" Lena looked just a little too cheerful as she spoke – like she was forcing it.

"Lena...please," Mike implored.

She sighed and refused to make eye contact with Mike. "Kristin really is fine. Actually...she's getting married."

Mike's heart stopped, and his stomach dropped to his toes. "Wh-what do you mean, she's getting married?"

"I mean," Lena finally lifted her head. "She met a man, she fell in love, and now they're getting married. I'm sorry, Mike."

Mike felt like a thousand needles were pricking his skin at once. "When? When is she getting married, Lena?"

Lena shifted uncomfortably. "Um...today."

The color drained from Mike's face. "Today? Where is she getting married? Lena, you have to tell me!"

"I don't know, honest!" Lena shook her head. "I couldn't get the day off since I'm so new here. I think it was some church downtown."

Mike tore out of the coffee shop back to his car.

"Mike!" Lena called after him. "Mike, this is a terrible idea!"

Mike tore through the streets of LA, madly searching on his phone for all the churches in the downtown area. He stopped at any and all he could find, peering in through the windows of some or bursting right through the doors of others. It was hopeless. There were so many churches; he would never find Kristin. Not in time, anyway.

Frustrated, defeated, feeling like he was going to break down any moment, Mike parked and sat down on a stairway to the side of a museum. *The Museum of Contemporary Art,* the sign said. He buried his head in his hands and tried to keep from screaming. He had waited too long. He tried to wait until everything in his life was perfect, but he missed his shot with Kristin because of it. He should have taken the chance.

"I'm sorry, Dad," Mike whispered to himself. A single tear trickled down his nose.

Just then, the doors of the museum burst open, and a huge crowd came pouring out. They separated into two rows on either side of the doors, blowing bubbles and cheering – they were attending a wedding.

Mike stood but watched from a distance as more and more people spilled out. Then, the bride and groom paraded through the crowd, laughing and clutching each other's hands.

The bride was Kristin.

Of course, Mike thought. *Of course, she would get married at an art museum. That's the perfect place for Kristin.*

Mike's heart pounded with the fury of a thunderstorm as he watched her dance through the bubbles with her new love. She was smiling, beaming with a radiant glow. She leaned her head against her new husband's shoulder and closed her eyes, satisfaction written all over her face.

Mike swallowed hard. She was so happy – wasn't that all he ever wanted? Even if it wasn't with him, didn't he want her to have the best life possible?

Mike closed his eyes and fought back the tears that threatened to spill over. *Yes, that's the chance I want her to have.*

He breathed deeply as he quietly watched Kristin get into a convertible with the love of her life. The groom honked, and Kristin waved, giggling with glee as the couple pulled away from the wedding guests.

As their car passed, Mike inadvertently made eye contact with Kristin. Time slowed down, almost to a standstill. Kristin's face melted from pure bliss to shock, to overwhelming sadness. Tears sprang into her eyes, and she covered her mouth as she looked right at Mike, standing on the steps where she had just married another man.

Mike smiled sadly at her and nodded his approval, hoping that Kristin would understand what he meant. As the car disappeared around the corner, he hung his head for a brief moment. Then, he took a deep breath and walked towards the museum, through the crowd of Kristin's wedding guests.

Mike felt an odd sense of peace and calm as he went inside, drinking in the art pieces that Kristin loved so much. He felt strongly that all would be well in his life, as painful as it may be in the present moment.

Some chances are worth taking – but most are worth giving to the ones you love.

LUTHER
You Make Me Feel Brand New

Luther Robinson grimaced as another stab of pain shot through his side. He grabbed his stomach and let out a low moan, bending in half at his desk. Sweat was starting to glisten on his forehead, and he was beginning to shake, the warning signs of a fever that he was choosing to ignore.

The window in his dorm room was wide open, letting a nighttime breeze float through the room. Luther slowly got up to shut it. He had wanted the fresh air to help him stay awake while he finished his term paper, but now it only made him feel worse. He wanted to avoid seeing a doctor at all costs – as a struggling college student, that was a cost he couldn't afford.

"Augh!" he collapsed onto the floor as another wave of pain wracked his body.

Maybe he would need that doctor after all. He managed to drag himself to his car and drive to Massachusetts General Hospital.

Luther was a student at Berklee College of Music in Boston, studying Music Education. He was a gentle, quiet man, who spent his time practicing piano and collecting minerals. He was born and raised in the

Roxbury neighborhood and had dreamed of going to Berklee to become a music teacher since he was in the sixth grade. His music teacher at that time, Mr. Sterling, had inspired Luther to pursue this path. Mr. Sterling would always say, "Music isn't just about notes on a page. It's about feeling feelings, it's about getting other people to feel feelings, and it's about adding beauty to the world."

Since then, Luther wanted to add beauty to the world in everything he did.

He limped into the ER of Mass. General to the check-in counter.

"Excuse me, ma'am? I'm in a lot of pain, and I need to see a doctor."

The nurse on the other side of the counter handed him a clipboard of forms to fill out.

He hobbled over to one of the chairs in the waiting room to complete them.

Name: Luther Robinson
Date of Birth: August 15th, 1981
Gender: Male
Race/Ethnicity: Black/African American

"Sir?" a nurse approached him just then. "Would you follow me, please? We have a bed waiting for you in the ER."

Luther followed her back through the halls, clutching his stomach the whole way.

A few minutes later, he was lying in a hospital bed in a backless cotton gown, with nothing but a thin privacy curtain separating him from a stranger in the next bed. The pain was getting worse, so he was glad that he left when he did.

A female voice came from the other side of the curtain.

"Mr. Robinson? May I come in?"

"Yeah sure," Luther called out weakly.

The curtain drew back, and a beautiful woman stepped through. She was gorgeous; Luther had never seen someone so lovely! Her soft, brown eyes held a warmth that made him feel instantly at ease, and her light smile made his heart flutter.

I'm going to marry her someday, he thought.

"Hi there, Mr. Robinson. My name is Katrina. I'm one of the nurses on duty, and I'll be taking care of you."

Luther tried to stammer out a few words, but Katrina's beauty and a stab of pain together rendered him speechless. He grimaced and grabbed at his side.

"Shh, that's alright. No need to talk now. Don't you worry. I'm going to get your vitals really quick then Dr. Henderson will be in to see you."

Katrina came up beside him and began checking his temperature, his oxygen levels, and blood pressure. Her every motion was graceful, every touch was soothing.

A few moments later, the doctor arrived.

"Hello, there! I'm Dr. Henderson. Nice to meet you, Mister..." he checked the clipboard in his hand, "Mr. Luther Robinson! Seems you're having some stomach pain, I see."

"His temp is up as well, Doctor," Katrina spoke from Luther's bedside.

"Thank you, Katrina. If you don't mind, Luther, I'm going to check out what's going on a little more." Dr. Henderson came over and examined Luther, pushing on his stomach and listening intently for when Luther gasped or grunted in pain.

"Well, my friend," Dr. Henderson began writing on his clipboard, "it appears that you have a nasty case of appendicitis; your appendix seems to be on the verge of bursting. We're going to get you into surgery rather quickly, so Katrina will get you ready, and I'll see you soon!" With a cheery wave, he turned and walked from the room.

Luther sat, stunned for a moment.

"Are you alright, Mr. Robinson?" Katrina asked.

Luther slowly nodded. "Yeah, it's just, um...it freaks you out when you hear that you're going into emergency surgery."

Katrina smiled gently and laid a hand on his shoulder. "I know it does, but it's really alright. Appendix surgeries are classified as 'emergency surgeries,' but they're very routine. And Dr. Henderson is one of the best doctors we have in the hospital. You're in good hands."

He turned to look her in the eye. "Will you be here when I get back?"

She laughed. "Yes, I will be."

"Then I know I'm in good hands for sure."

He didn't believe it, but Luther could have sworn that Katrina blushed before she turned away and busied herself with his IV.

LUTHER
I Can't Help Myself

A week later, Luther stood at the entrance of Mass. General once again. This time, his appendix was not bursting, and he stood tall and proud, not doubled over in pain. In his hands were a bouquet of flowers and a card. He took a deep breath to calm his nerves and stepped inside.

At the Information Desk, a rather sour-looking woman rolled back her glass window and met him with a cold stare. "May I help you?" she asked in a nasal voice.

"Hi there, yes, um…I was here last week. I got my appendix removed, you see, real exciting stuff, but uh…I want to say thank you to the nurse that treated me. And the doctor, too," he added hastily.

She eyed the flowers in his hand then turned to her computer with a sniff. "What was the name?"

"Katrina."

The woman rolled her eyes. "What's Katrina's last name? It's a big hospital; there are probably dozens of Katrinas in my system."

"Uhh…" Luther froze. He hadn't thought this far ahead. He didn't know Katrina's last name, not even a guess. How would he ever find her?

"Mr. Robinson?" a familiar, sweet voice said behind him.

He turned to see Katrina standing with a cup of coffee in her hand and a puzzled smile on her face.

His own face broke into a wide grin as the grumpy Information Desk woman slammed her window closed behind him.

"Hi!" he said.

She laughed. "Hi, how are you doing? Are your stitches alright?"

"Oh, yeah, yeah, my stitches are great! Um, these are for you." He thrust the flowers out towards her.

Katrina's giggle made his heart skip a beat. "Well, thank you, these are beautiful. And here I thought they were for Dr. Henderson."

Luther snickered then anxiously tugged at his ear. "I um...I actually wanted to ask you something, too."

"Oh?"

"Would you...ah, actually here," he said as he handed over a card to her. "Just read this."

Katrina shook her head with a smile and opened the small note card.

*Roses are red, violets are blue, my appendix is gone, but I'm so glad
I met you.
Would you like to go to dinner with me?*

—Luther

"Oh, Mr. Robinson..." Katrina breathed.

As the words left her mouth, Luther swore the sun shone brighter, the birds outside sang louder, the music in his heart rose to a crescendo—

"No."

Luther blinked. "Um...what?"

Katrina smiled sadly. "I'm sorry, Mr. Robinson You're incredibly sweet, but sometimes patients get feelings for their nurses just because they were vulnerable and we took care of them. Do you think that could be what's happening here?"

Luther shook his head, forcefully. "No, I don't think that's it at all and call me Luther, please. I think you're sweet, compassionate, and...

rather beautiful." He chuckled nervously. "And I'd really like to take you to dinner sometime."

She smiled again. "Thank you, Luther, that's very kind. But I'm sorry, my answer is still no. I do appreciate the flowers, though." She buried her nose into one of the yellow daisies and breathed deeply. "These are my favorite. I have to go clock in now, okay?" She gestured to the nurse's station that was right down the hall.

He only nodded.

"Okay. Bye, Luther. Thank you again." She turned and went to start her shift.

The window behind Luther slid open again, and the grumpy woman stuck her head out. "Well, that could have gone better."

* * *

Luther came back two days later at noon with a bouquet made entirely of yellow daisies. He left them with one of the nurses at the nurse's station where he had met Katrina the last time, with another card attached.

You said that yellow daisies were your favorite. I hope you meant it!
Reconsider dinner?

—Luther

He also wrote his phone number at the bottom this time.

That evening, his phone chimed with a text. His heart skipped a beat when he saw it was Katrina. She thanked him for the daisies and said yes, they were her favorite flower and that he was so sweet for remembering. She didn't say anything about dinner, and Luther decided not to push the issue.

Until the next day.

He went back to the hospital with another bouquet of yellow daisies, at noon again. This time, he didn't leave a card but left a box of cookies from a local bakery.

A few hours later, his phone chimed with another text from Katrina!

"*Cookies were amazing!!*" she wrote. "*No time for a lunch break, so they kept me going. Thanks!*"

Luther wrote back, "*You're welcome! So... dinner?*"

He waited what seemed like an hour before the reply came from Katrina: "*Hmmm... I'll think about it. ;-)*"

Luther smiled as he read her words. It wasn't exactly a yes, but it wasn't a no! And now he knew his next step in the quest for Katrina's heart.

The following day, at his regular time of noon, Luther marched into the hospital with his standard bouquet of yellow daisies and a boxed lunch from the deli down the street. If Katrina didn't have time to get real food on her breaks, Luther would make sure she had some waiting for whenever she needed it.

This same song and dance continued for the next two weeks. He was brimming with confidence every time. He strode to that hospital every day like he was a superstar. Every day right at exactly 12 noon, Luther brought a boxed lunch and a bouquet of yellow daisies to the hospital for Katrina. Every day, she would text him to say thank you but would dismiss his proposals for a dinner date.

Until one day...

Two weeks to the day he first brought her flowers, Luther walked into the hospital to see Katrina standing at the nurse's station, arms crossed. He stopped in his tracks then slowly shuffled towards her, holding out the flowers as a sort of peace offering.

"Hey," he said with a soft smile. He had forgotten how much her eyes dazzled him.

She just shook her head at him, a smirk on her face. "When are you going to learn that I'll just keep saying no?"

"Well," Luther grinned, "when are you going to learn that I'll just keep asking until you say yes?"

Katrina laughed, much to his relief, and smacked his arm playfully. "You really are persistent, aren't you?"

Luther shrugged. "It's easy to be persistent when you're certain of what it is you want."

This drew a sigh from Katrina. "Alright, Luther, I'll tell you what: no one has ever bought me fourteen lunches in a row before. It's the sweetest, most diligent, craziest thing a man has done to get my attention. But damn, did you get it. I think that warrants more of a thank you than just a text."

She stepped closer to him, looking up into his eyes. Luther felt like he was on fire; he was just going to melt into a puddle right here in the hall.

"Yes," she said.

Luther's breath caught in his throat. "What?"

Katrina grinned, "I said yes, Luther. I'd like to go to dinner with you. Now don't make me say it again!"

He burst into gleeful laughter and scooped Katrina up in a giant bear hug, sweeping her off the floor and twirling her around.

"I am going to give you the best date you have ever seen," he promised solemnly. "I swear."

Katrina laughed with him and hugged him tightly. "I'm sure that you will, Luther. I'm sure you will."

LUTHER
Ain't No Woman Like The One I Got

Their first date was the best date that either of them had ever experienced. Until their second date trumped it. And their third one beat that. And so on, and on, and on.

Katrina and Luther were going steady within a week. Within a month, they were madly in love. While Luther had given up his daily deliveries to Katrina, he still made it a point to bring her a boxed lunch and a single yellow daisy every Saturday when Katrina worked first shift. He would wait by the nurse's station while she whizzed by, rushing from patient to patient. When she finally had a moment to breathe, he would deliver the food and the flower directly into her hands with a kiss.

Three months into their relationship, Luther graduated from Berklee with a Master's Degree in Music Education. Katrina made sure that she had the day off to be there and cheer him on. Katrina was the only one that he had now; Luther's father had left when he was just two years old, and his mother had passed away in his freshman year of college.

During the ceremony, Katrina applauded fiercely, cheered exuberantly, and took dozens of pictures as he walked across the stage to accept his diploma. Luther's heart ached in a mixture of joy and grief – how he wished his mother could be here to see this, but it was also glorious was to have Katrina by his side. In his heart, he knew that his mother was smiling down on the two of them.

As the graduates poured out of the building afterward, he spotted Katrina through the crowd, waiting for him. In her hands – a bouquet of yellow daisies and a boxed lunch.

Luther laughed heartily as he scooped her up in his arms. "What's this about, Miss Murray?"

She giggled as she squeezed him back. "Well, you never told me what your favorite flowers were, so I had to go with what I knew. As for the lunch," she grew serious and looked him straight in the eye, "you listen to me, Luther Robinson. You support me every day, every week, every rough shift, and every good one. But today, I'm flipping the script; today is all about me supporting you. You've accomplished something extraordinary. I want you to know that. Your Mama would be so incredibly proud of you. I'm proud of you too, honey, and I…" She drew in a deep breath. "I love you."

Luther wrapped his arms around her and held her close as silent tears leaked from his eyes. He had hoped that Mama would be proud of him, but hearing it spoken out loud by somebody else tore at his heart. And Katrina just said she loved him! While their relationship was a blazing inferno of passion, that was the first time that either of them had said those words.

"I love you too, Katrina," he whispered hoarsely. "Oh *god*, do I love you."

* * *

Right after graduation, Luther secured a job as a substitute teacher at a local middle school. He moved off Berklee's campus and into an apartment with Katrina, close to the hospital but further from his work. He didn't mind. She worked so hard, and he wanted her to have the most comfortable commute possible, the safest commute possible.

He continued to bring her lunch every Saturday (with a side of yellow daisies), and sometimes she would have enough time to take a proper lunch break and eat with him in the cafeteria. At night, when Katrina wasn't working, they would snuggle up on the couch and watch their favorite TV shows...sometimes just Katrina's favorite TV shows.

"Ugh, they made *another* season of this?" Luther would moan.

Katrina would smack him playfully, "Luther, you got lucky and found a woman that was willing to deal with your crazy self. Other dudes aren't so fortunate."

Then she would turn back and nuzzle into his chest as the television came to life. "*Tonight, the most dramatic season of 'The Bachelor' begins...*"

Luther would sigh and wrap his arms around her, pretending to hate every minute of the show.

They had their routine down; it was all figured out. Every moment was perfect with Katrina. Sure, they had their squabbles, but they always ended the same way: apologies and kisses under the bedsheets. They were madly in love, and Luther wanted things to stay this way forever.

So, one day, Luther drove to her parents' house in the suburbs. Alone.

He had met Mr. and Mrs. Murray several times before. They were lovely people, who were proud of their daughter and wanted the best life for her. Luther agreed with this sentiment, so they had gotten along splendidly thus far. But today felt different. Today, there was a tension in his heart as he brushed off his jacket and walked up the brick stairway to the front door. He inhaled deeply as he rang the doorbell.

Mrs. Murray answered. "Luther!" she said with a surprised smile. "Come in! We weren't expecting you today. Is everything alright?"

He stepped inside as she closed the door behind him. "Hello, Mrs. Murray. Everything is fine. I'm sorry to surprise you. Katrina is at work, but I wanted to speak with you and Mr. Murray. Do you have a few minutes?"

The Murrays and Luther gathered in the living room. Mr. Murray shook Luther's hand before sitting down. They went through the polite chit-chat; how's work, how's the business, how's the golf game, how 'bout the Patriots' lineup this year...the usual topics of conversation. Then there was a lull, and Luther knew that the moment had come.

He wiped his sweating palms on his knees. "Well, the reason I came to talk to you today is...well, um...sorry I had a whole thing prepared, and now I'm blanking." He chuckled nervously then cleared his throat and sat up in his chair. "Look, I love your daughter very much. She's an angel, not just to me but to all her patients and coworkers. She's a special human being. I know that for a fact, and I want to spend the rest of my life taking care of her." He shifted in his seat and took a deep breath. "Mr. Murray, Mrs. Murray – I'd like to ask your daughter to marry me, and I'm here to ask you for your blessing."

Mrs. Murray gasped, and tears glistened in her eyes as her hands flew to her face. Mr. Murray hadn't moved a muscle except for a slow smile that was spreading across his face.

"Oh Luther, of course—" Mrs. Murray started to say, but Mr. Murray interrupted.

"Now, hold on just a minute. You're asking for our only daughter's hand in marriage."

"Yes, sir." Luther nodded solemnly.

"Well," a twinkle shone in his eye, "I feel like that warrants some consideration, now doesn't it?"

"Uh, ye-yes, sir," Luther stammered.

Mr. Murray leaned forward in his chair, resting his elbows on his knees. "You love my daughter, you say."

"Yes, sir. Very much."

"You plan to give her a good life?"

"Of course, sir."

"You promise to take care of her and make sure she is happy, comfortable, able to pursue all her dreams?"

Luther nodded vigorously. "Yes sir, I do promise. I want her to be happy more than I want anything else in the world. I would give my life for her to be happy."

Mr. Murray leaned back, a smile on his face and mist in his eyes.

"Well, Luther, I think that is a bit extreme considering you make her happier than I've seen in a long time. Of course, you have our blessing, son. We would love to have you in our family."

* * *

Katrina eagerly said, "Yes," when Luther proposed. Actually, she said something more along the lines of "*EEEEK!*" which Luther took as a "yes" anyway.

They got married soon afterward, a beautiful October wedding in Boston. It was a small ceremony in a beautiful park, with just Katrina's family, some of Luther's relatives, and their close friends. For their reception, they all went out to eat at a small burger joint. It was informal and fun, but it was perfect for the happy couple.

One year later, the day after their first wedding anniversary, Luther found himself rushing to the hospital again. This time, it wasn't him who was in pain – it was Katrina. But her pain was not because of appendicitis. This pain had been nine months in the making, and now it had finally reached its peak.

Twelve hours later, their beautiful daughter, Kendra Grace Robinson, was born into the world.

LUTHER
Isn't She Lovely

Fifteen Years Later

"Kendra!" Luther thundered from the bottom of the stairs. "It's time for school. Let's move!"

No answer.

He sighed and rubbed his temples. He wondered whether he could afford a boarding school next year, somewhere rather far away. He loved his daughter dearly, but 15-year-old girls were a beast of their own kind.

He made his way up the stairs to Kendra's bedroom, where loud music was thumping through the door. Luther pounded his fist on the door.

"Kendra!" he called again. "Sweetheart, I'm sure your makeup is just fine. We gotta go now!"

Still no response.

Luther sighed. "I'm gonna regret this..." he mumbled to himself. He shoved the door open and stepped into Kendra's room.

Kendra, his 15-year-old daughter, stood in front of a full-length mirror. She wore a tiny yellow crop top, a distressed denim miniskirt, and four-inch wedge sandals on her feet. Her makeup was done heavily, with long wings of eyeliner and bold lipstick, and Luther could barely recognize the youthful face of his baby girl.

She whipped around when she caught sight of him in the mirror. "Oh my god, *Dad!* Get out of my *room!*"

He tried to swallow a mixture of fear and anger that was rising in his throat. "Do not tell me you're wearing that to school today. No way, you get changed right now, young lady!"

"What? No, my clothes are fine! I have to dress like this. It's building my brand!"

Luther couldn't help snorting. "Your *brand?* Kendra, you are 15 years old. Where did you get this idea of your *brand?*"

Kendra rolled her eyes dramatically. "Ugh, you wouldn't get it. All the modeling agencies I follow on the gram say to live your brand every day if you want to make it in the industry."

"The modeling industry, you mean?"

"Yes, duh."

"Well, you'll have plenty of time to build this 'brand' of yours, at least three years. We've already talked about this. You are way too young to be getting into that kind of stuff, Kendra! You know what these people do on these accounts? They make promises to young girls, who don't know any better, and get them into terrible situations!" Luther couldn't help that his voice was getting louder.

"God, it's not your decision anyway!" Kendra flung her arms into the air in frustration. "I'm my own person, Dad! If I want to be a model, I'm going to be a model! You can't control me!"

"Ha! On the contrary, my dear daughter, you live under the roof that I own, in a room that I own, and you sleep on a bed that I own. So, by proxy, I do own you!"

"*GET...OUT!*" Kendra screamed. She pushed Luther out of the room and slammed the door.

Luther buried his face in his hands and moaned as the music in Kendra's room cranked up even louder.

He lifted his head when he heard a noise coming from the master bedroom. He went inside to find Katrina sitting on the floor of the master bathroom in front of the toilet.

"Hey, hey..." he said softly as he rushed to her side. "What's going on, baby?"

She smiled weakly, "Oh, it's just some of that leftover Chinese food I had last night, back for vengeance."

"Do you need to call off work? You should stay home, really, Kat."

She shook her head, swatting his hand away as she stood. "No, Luther. I'm fine. No fever, it's just a little vomit. And I need to go in anyway. We're short-staffed like crazy. The girls would kill me if I called out."

"Well, only if you're sure." Luther brought over a set of scrubs from the closet. "But if you feel sick again, you call me that very minute, and I'll come by and get you, alright?"

"Yeah, yeah..." Katrina said with a wink. "Now you and our Next Top Model need to get going. You're going to be late."

Luther sighed. He kissed Katrina goodbye and walked back to the lion's den.

* * *

Luther and Kendra drove to school together every morning. Luther would drop her off at the doors of the high school before making the short drive up the hill to the middle school where he taught music. This was their routine since Kendra was in sixth grade. Luther typically loved this time with his daughter, driving to and from school. They would talk about their days, make up parodies of songs on the radio, then laugh at how bad they sounded.

Lately, though, it had been different. Ever since Kendra started her sophomore year of high school, things just felt...different. First, she stopped laughing at her dad's parodies and would roll her eyes instead. Then, she stopped tolerating it altogether and asked him to stop. Now, it was getting to the point where they didn't talk at all. She just sat in the passenger seat with her earbuds in, staring at the phone in her hand, blocking him out.

It made Luther angry, but more than that, it hurt his heart. He missed those precious moments with his little girl.

"Hey, Kendra?" he said to her.

She couldn't hear him over the music playing in her earbuds.

"Helloooo, Kendra." He waved his hand to try to get her attention, but she was engrossed in her phone.

At the next red light, Luther leaned over just far enough to peer at her phone screen.

His stomach lurched.

Kendra had Instagram opened on her phone, and she was in her messages on the app. Luther could see the username @model_service_nyc – and a picture of Kendra wearing a thin bikini.

He reached over and yanked the phone out of her hands.

"What the hell?!" she screeched as she yanked out her earbuds.

"What the hell is right, Kendra! What the hell is this on your phone? Why are you sending pictures like this to people on the internet?"

"Gosh, Dad, it's an agency! They're based in New York; they need to see samples of my work!" she scrambled to take the phone back from him.

"Like hell, it's an agency! They want photos they should ask for a portfolio, not this! What the heck are you thinking?"

The light turned green; Luther chirped the tires pulling forward. The school was just ahead now. He simultaneously wanted this car ride to be over already but had so much more to say to his daughter.

Kendra was still fighting to grab the phone. "Dad, give me my phone back! I need it!"

"No, Kendra, you don't need it. You need food, you need water, you need some goddam sense, but you *don't* need this phone!" He threw it angrily into the compartment on the driver's side door.

Kendra was crying now as they pulled up to the school's entrance. "Dad, I need my phone, please."

"You'll get your phone tonight after I've deleted all these apps."

"Are you serious right now? I need my phone! What if there's an emergency?"

"Oh, like what? You realize you're not wearing a whole shirt?"

Kendra's eyes flashed, and even under all her makeup, her face turned red. "Screw you!" she screamed as she flung the car door open.

"Bye, honey! Love you too!" Luther called sarcastically.

"I *hate* you!" Kendra slammed the car door shut, hard enough to rattle the whole vehicle. She stormed off towards her group of friends, who instantly flocked around her like twittering birds and shot Luther nasty looks through the windshield as Kendra sobbed.

Great, he slumped over the steering wheel with a huge sigh. Not even 8 am, and he was already exhausted, physically, mentally, emotionally. He wished this day could just be over. Or better yet, he could go back in time and start all over. *Well, tomorrow will be another day to get it right.*

The car behind him honked, just a polite beep, to ask him to pull forward. Luther sat up and waved an apology before slowly rolling towards the middle school.

LUTHER
Overjoyed

Luther sighed and checked his watch: 8:15 pm. He stretched then continued to straighten up the music room. It was almost spring concert time, and that meant extra rehearsals after school. A labor of love that he genuinely didn't mind; it had just been a long day.

He went to his desk and checked his phone. Thirteen missed calls from Katrina. He groaned. More than likely, Kendra had come home in a fit after the fight they had, and Katrina was furious with his actions. Not that she sided with Kendra all the time, but in her words, "You're the daddy, better act like it."

He pinched the bridge of his nose between his fingers as he redialed her number.

She answered on the first ring, "Hey, babe."

"Hey, honey. Look, I'm sorry for how I handled Kendra today. I'm sure she's already told you, but Kat if you would have seen— "

"Luther," Katrina interrupted him, "we can get to that in a minute. We have something more important to discuss first."

Luther blinked. "More...more important than me screaming at our daughter?"

She laughed. "Oh baby, I wanted to wait to tell you in person, but I just couldn't! I have to tell you now before I bust! Luther – I'm pregnant."

Luther didn't breathe for a moment.

"Honey? You still there?"

"No, you're not."

Katrina laughed gleefully again. "Yes, I am! I got checked out after work today, and it's official. Read it and weep, baby!"

Tears began to form in Luther's eyes. "But it's been so long since Kendra. And the doctors said it wasn't likely after those tests…"

"Well, they were wrong, baby. They were dead wrong. We got another baby on the way."

It finally sank in, and Luther succumbed to the tears. "Kat, that's amazing! I can't believe this; we've got another Robinson coming! Oh, baby girl, I love you so much, I really do!"

Katrina was sniffling on the other end of the line. "Well, get your butt home so we can celebrate!"

Luther laughed. "I will, I'm leaving right now! I'm coming home, babe. I'm coming home."

* * *

Moments later, Luther happily drummed on the steering wheel as he drove. His favorite song played on the radio. He rolled the windows down and enjoyed the nighttime wind on his face, just like that fateful night when he went to the hospital and met the love of his life. Something so terrible had turned so wonderful in the blink of an eye.

He stopped at Parkway Shop, a convenience store and gas station, to pick up chocolate and, of course, yellow daisies for Katrina. Parkway Shop was the same place where Luther had bought all those bouquets of yellow daisies for her years ago; it only seemed fitting to get them here again.

He walked inside with a bounce to his step. The cashier, Mr. Choudhry, greeted him as he came through the doors.

"Evening, Mr. Robinson!" he said with a wave.

"How are you doing, Mr. Choudhry? You guys got any yellow daisies I can take off your hands?"

The cashier's face lit up. "Of course! It is a special occasion for Mrs. Robinson, yes?"

Luther leaned on the counter. "For both of us, good sir. After all this time...we've got another little one on the way."

Mr. Choudhry threw his hands up in the air with a cry! He ran around the counter to where Luther was standing and wrapped him up in a giant hug. "Oh, my friend, that is wonderful news! I will give you my discount, yes? Choose whatever chocolates you like! Take the big box!"

"What's all that commotion about, huh?" a gruff voice came from the back of the store. Tom, the owner of Parkway Shop, poked his head around the corner. He grinned when he saw Luther. Luther had frequented his store even since the tradition of the yellow daisies had become less frequent, and he was one of Tom's favorite customers, though Tom would never admit that he had a favorite anything.

"Mr. Thomas, Mr. Thomas! Our friend is expecting a baby!" Mr. Choudhry bounced on his tiptoes in excitement.

"Well! That so, Luther? Congratulations!" He came over and clapped Luther on the back. "You had better get some of them yellow daisies for the Missus, huh? Tell you what, pick out anything you'd like. It's on the house. Don't tell anyone else, Choudhry."

Luther exchanged glances with Mr. Choudhry, who smiled and winked.

"Thank you very much, Thomas. It's very kind of you." Luther shook his hand and grinned. "I'm glad that I could tell you in person. Only seems right after all this time. It's good to celebrate with friends, too."

Thomas grunted in response. "Well, don't just dawdle there. Get something good and get home." He waved Luther off, suspiciously rubbing his eye as he walked away.

Luther picked the biggest bunch of yellow daisies he could find and the biggest heart-shaped box of chocolates. Mr. Choudhry smiled and gave him a thumbs up. As Luther exited the store, he turned and shouted a final thank-you to Thomas, who was still restocking some shelves in the back of the store.

When Luther got to his car, he realized that he was almost out of gas. *At least I noticed here and not down the road.* He waited for a group of men to pass then backed his car into a pump spot. He waited as the tank filled, humming as he did.

POP, POP, POP!

Luther's head whipped around. Those were gunshots! And they were coming from the store!

BANG! BANG!

Luther started for the store's entrance. Just then, he saw the group of men that had passed by his car earlier, now running out of the store. One held a register drawer in his hands, with loose bills and coins spilling from the sides as he fled — the other clutched a couple boxes of cigarettes to his chest. The third and final man carried nothing, except for a glinting handgun that he waved through the air as he ran.

Tom came bursting out of the doors at that moment, brandishing a shotgun. His face was as pale as a sheet, but his jaw was set. He aimed at the robbers and unleashed some rounds: *BANG! BANG! BANG!*

He paused to reload. Seeing Luther, he scurried over to meet him. "Choudhry's hurt. You go help him out while I deal with these assholes." He ran towards his truck to chase down the group in their getaway vehicle.

As the two men parted ways, an older woman hid inside her car, unseen at one of the gas pumps. With shaking hands, she dialed: 9-1-1.

LUTHER
Through The Fire

Luther ran inside the store, panting, looking wildly around him for Mr. Choudhry. He saw the cashier's feet peeking out from behind the corner of the counter.

"Oh, God..." Luther breathed as he scrambled to reach the injured man.

He saw a bloody mess on the floor in front of him. Choudhry had been hit by one of the bullets, luckily in the upper arm, but was losing a lot of blood. Luther frantically tried to remember the lessons Katrina had taught him about arteries and blood pressure and tourniquets...

"Mr. Robinson," Choudhry coughed out weakly, "you must go to your family. Go home, Mr. Robinson. It's not safe here."

Luther shook his head vehemently as tears stung his eyes. He forced a smile for his bleeding friend. "No way, Mr. Choudhry. You're stuck with me, alright? I'm going to take good care of you. Don't you worry. I'll even give you my discount." He winked, and Mr. Choudhry wheezed out a laugh. "Now, this might hurt a bit. I'm sorry about that. Just stay with me."

All of a sudden, he heard a noise in an aisle next to the refrigerators.

"Thomas got one of them in the back. He might still be alive," he said weakly.

Luther quickly got up on his feet and headed back slowly. He recognized one of the men who came in earlier. He was on the ground, but he was struggling to his feet. He had a wound on his torso. He groaned weakly. He was clutching a small gun in his hand and pointed it towards Luther. With a burst of speed, Luther tackled him, and the gun flew out of his hand. He stopped moving. He wasn't sure if he was still alive or not, so he took his gun just in case. The priority right now was to stop Mr. Choudhry's bleeding.

Luther took off his button-down shirt, leaving only his tank top undershirt covering his body. He ripped the button-down into strips, then into some larger pieces as well. The long strips he used to tie a tourniquet around Choudhry's arm, just below the shoulder where the major artery was, to slow the blood flow to his injury. The other pieces he bundled together to make a giant bandage with some leftover. Luther pressed them to the gunshot wound in Choudhry's arm.

Choudhry hissed in pain but did not move. Luther slowly applied more pressure to help stop the bleeding. In the back of his mind, he wondered if Thomas was alright and if the robbers had gotten away... if Katrina wondered where he was.

Minutes passed; Choudhry's bleeding did not slow down. Luther's hands were completely covered, his knees were soaked from kneeling in the puddles, and splatters freckled his shirt like confetti from a sick parade. He knew that Mr. Choudhry would need more medical attention than Luther could give to him. They needed an ambulance, and they needed it soon.

He patted his pockets, searching for his phone. *Shit.* It was still in his car parked outside. He strained to see if there was a phone behind the counter — no such luck. He remembered that they didn't have a landline.

"Mr. Choudhry?" he turned to his friend to ask if he had his phone.

Mr. Choudhry had passed out from blood loss, his face a gray color, his eyes closed. Panicked, Luther felt for a pulse – it was there, but it was weak. There wasn't time; he had to call for help now!

He scrambled to his feet and ran for the door. He took two steps outside before stopping dead in his tracks. Luther felt his heart stop. He felt his stomach twist into a thousand knots. He felt a rush of fear like he had never felt before.

About a dozen police officers surrounded the store, all of them had their guns drawn.

All their barrels were pointing right at him.

* * *

No, Luther thought. *No, this is all a mistake. They can help Mr. Choudhry. They're here for him.*

"Put your hands in the air!" an officer shouted from somewhere in the sea of blue uniforms.

"Please," Luther called out. "Please, there's a man inside. He needs— "

"Drop the gun and put your hands in the air NOW! Do it!"

Startled, Luther scolded himself for stupidly bringing the gun with him. He did as he was told and dropped the gun. He quickly raised his hands and spread his fingers. He pleaded for help again. "Sir, I need your help! There's a man— "

"Don't speak!" the same voice yelled. Luther still couldn't discern which officer to whom the voice belonged. "Don't say a single word! Now get on the ground on your knees!"

Luther sputtered, "On my knees?"

"*DO IT!* Do it now, or I'll shoot!"

His heart leaped into his throat. His stomach threatened to hurl. He had never heard those words before; they were horrifying.

Slowly yet shakily, Luther lowered himself onto his knees, hands still raised in the air. He felt moisture on his knees and dared to glance down at them.

It was only at that moment he realized – he was covered in Mr. Choudhry's blood. Absolutely covered.

Luther knew that it was because he was helping Mr. Choudhry. Footage from security cameras would show them as much. But at this moment, these officers didn't know that, and they were too afraid of him to consider the possibility. All they saw was a black man in a blood-spattered tank top at the scene of a crime. And that was enough to cause the tip of every gun to be trained on Luther's chest.

He swallowed another bout of panic that was rising in his throat. For so many years, he had endured the seemingly-passive racism that reared its ugly head in his daily life: the extra once-overs by the grocery store clerk, the unprovoked traffic stops, the white ladies clutching their purses tight. Now, in a culmination of all those little moments, the poignant, bitter truth of what it meant to be a black man in America was staring him right in the face – in the form of a dozen 9mm police-issue pistols.

He wanted more than anything to scream and beg for mercy but knew that would be one of the worst things he could do. So, he remained silent, wide-eyed, terrified…covered in another man's blood.

The officer's voice broke into his thoughts. "Now lower yourself to your stomach on the ground! DO NOT reach behind you! DO NOT move your hands from out of our sight! If you do, WE WILL SHOOT! Do you understand?"

Tear sprang into Luther's eyes, blurring his vision, and choking off his words, so he only nodded and slowly began to lower himself like he was told. He thought of Katrina, how she would tell him to be calm, just do as they say and it will all be over. He thought of Kendra, his little girl who needed her daddy to protect her. He thought of his unborn child – oh, how he loved that baby already! He had to be strong. He had to be calm; it was the only way he would get home to his family.

Suddenly, a sharp blow landed on his back, causing Luther to see stars with the amount of pain he felt. He fell to the ground as three police officers swarmed around him.

LUTHER
Ain't No Love

Luther coughed and struggled to regain his breath. His arms were roughly yanked behind him, and handcuffs snapped across his wrists.

"Please..." he groaned.

"Shut up!" the same officer's voice rang out. A blow landed on Luther's face. His vision cleared as the officer kneeled to look him in the eyes. His pupils were dilated, and he was breathing heavily.

He leaned in close and growled, "Thought you could get away with it all, huh? Thought you could just injure an innocent man, swipe a little spending money and walk free, go on your merry little way? Think again, you piece of shit." He landed another punch on Luther's face.

Luther cried out and writhed in pain.

"Stop resisting!" the officer boomed. He began to land more kicks and punches on Luther's body. The other two officers jumped on top of Luther and wrangled him like he was a thrashing animal, twisting his legs and arms, throwing punches all the while.

Luther sobbed. He went limp and made up his mind that he would just take the abuse until they'd had enough, only then would he speak.

He would explain everything, and he would tell them what really happened. Where was Thomas? Thomas would tell them! Dear God, please let him be here!

His eyes roamed the parking lot. All he could see were flashing blue and red lights in the night sky. He felt the officers kneel on top of his body, and his vision began to fade.

* * *

An officer came rushing out of the store. "Man down! Middle Eastern or Asian male, about mid-forties, gunshot wound to the arm!"

More officers ran to join him in treating Mr. Choudhry, but the two officers on Luther's back didn't budge. The officer who had led the charge against him leaned down to speak again. Luther could barely make out the name on his badge, *Smyth*.

"Your victim, eh?" Smyth smirked at him. "Got in your way, did he? Shame on him."

"Please," Luther grunted through his tears. "Please, I can't breathe."

"Ha!" Smyth slapped his knee. "Boy, these are the two lightweights of the precinct! That ain't nothing for a big guy like you!"

"Sir! Sir, I can't breathe!"

A cry for help that should have elicited compassion instead pissed off Officer Smyth. His brow furrowed, and his face turned red. "Shut up! You're fine. Now just shut up!"

One of the officers seemed to be uncomfortable with the turn of events and stepped forward. "Sergeant, he's not resisting! There's no need to do that."

"Shut it, rookie. This is how we do things here," said Smyth.

He pushed one of the other officers aside and knelt on top of Luther himself. His knee dug right into the side of Luther's neck, choking off Luther's voice even more than it already was, more than it ever should have been.

"Sergeant, this is not right. He's handcuffed and not able to resist. If you don't stop this, I'll file a formal complaint against you!"

Smyth grinned. "No one here will corroborate your story, rookie. If you don't shut up, everyone here will say that you did this," he said and suddenly stomped on Luther. The other shook his head and remained silent.

"Please! Please!" was all that Luther could muster. Images of his family began to flash through his mind. Kendra, the most beautiful girl in the world, the day that she was born. Her fourth birthday. Their rides to school in the morning. The fight they had earlier that day. He would do anything to take it all back now – to tell her that he loved her one more time.

He saw Katrina's precious face. The night they met in the hospital. His graduation day, her standing with the yellow daisies. Watching television together, curled up on the couch. The first night they brought Kendra home. He could hear her voice on the phone from just an hour ago, *"Get your butt home...come home..."*

Luther cried out as best he could through the pressure on his throat and the stream of tears, "I'm coming, baby! Kat! I'm coming! I'm coming home!"

"I said, SHUT UP!" Officer Smyth dug his knee further into Luther's neck.

"Katrina, I love you..." Luther sobbed quietly.

He could see another face in his mind now. A face that he hadn't seen in a long time but pictured often. A face that his heart could never forget.

"Mama?" he whispered.

The vision of his mother came into focus. She was smiling at him, though tears were streaming down her face. Her arms reached out for him. *"Hey, baby,"* he heard her say. *"Come on now; it'll be alright. Just come on over to me, Luther. It will all be okay. Your Mama's here now."*

"Mama," Luther whimpered. His soft tone grew louder as his mother seemed to draw closer to him. "Mama...oh, Mama, I can't breathe! Mama! Mama, please! I'm coming, Mama! *MAMA!*"

"That's it!" Officer Smyth hollered. He whipped his baton from his belt and slammed it down on Luther's temple.

Everything went dark. Then, Luther felt Mama's arms wrap him up in a warm embrace.

***

Thomas pulled back into the parking lot and jumped out of his truck and left his shotgun inside. "Did the one I shot get back up again?" he called out to an officer standing nearby.

"Who are you, sir?"

"I'm Thomas Wilkes, the owner of this store."

"Ah, my apologies, Mr. Wilkes. We have two injured in the store, and we have detained a suspect just over there." He gestured over to a group of police officers kneeling on top of a man on the ground.

Tom stopped in horror. His heart dropped to his stomach when he saw who they had actually detained.

Luther.

He was face-down on the ground, two police officers kneeling on his back, one awfully close to his neck. Blood could be seen on his pant legs, his arms, and fresh blood now oozed from his nose.

Thomas flew into a panic. "NO! Stop, get off of him! Are you crazy? Get off of him, right now, damn it!" He ran towards Luther.

Other police officers stepped in his path, blocking him from going any further. "Sir, we have detained one of the suspects; we're simply waiting for the paramedics to come treat the victim."

"He *is* the victim!" Thomas thundered. "He hasn't done a thing. He's innocent!"

"Sir, there is an injured man inside. He had a gun. We just have to take the necessary precautions—"

"I know there's an injured man inside; I'm the one who asked Luther to help him! Oh...oh, God, oh no, Luther. Luther, I'm so sorry!" Tom began to wail. He forced his way through the wall of police officers and collapsed on the ground next to Luther as they scrambled to restrain him.

Their faces were so close they could have touched. "Luther! Luther, can you hear me? Oh, God, Luther, I am so sorry. I am so sorry. I never meant for any of this to happen. I shouldn't have asked you to help. I'm so sorry."

Luther softly wheezed, so quietly that Thomas could barely make out his words: "Tho…mas…."

Tom gave in to the sobs that were threatening to wrack his body. "I'm sorry, Luther…I'm so sorry…" Tom cried tears of grief and fear as the officers dragged him away from Luther.

An ambulance pulled up at that moment. Four EMTs jumped from the vehicle and ran over to the spot where Luther was pinned to the ground.

"There's an injured man inside. This is the perp," Officer Smyth said. The officer behind him cleared their throat, and Smyth rolled his eyes. "Excuse me, *suspected* perp."

Two EMTs ran inside, and two stayed behind.

"What are you doing? I said there's an injured man inside!" Smyth bellowed.

"Well sir," one of the EMTs spoke as he pulled on his gloves. "Quite frankly, there's an injured man right here, too. 'Perp' or not, it's my duty to treat him. I see that he's handcuffed *and* unconscious, so could you please get off and allow me to do my job?"

Smyth scowled but obliged.

The EMT knelt down to take Luther's pulse. He put an ear to Luther's mouth, and his eyes flew up to Officer Smyth. "Uncuff this man, right now!"

"What? No way, he's dangerous!"

The EMT fumed, his ears turning a bright red. "Officer, this man is not breathing! I can't perform *life-saving* CPR with his hands bound behind his back, so will you please uncuff him?!"

"Shit…" Officer Smyth fumbled with the keys to the handcuffs.

The EMT rolled Luther over onto his back and began chest compressions. The other EMT began preparing the AED.

A minute passed; there was no change. The EMT's cut Luther's shirt down the middle and prepared him for the AED.

"Clear!" Luther's body contracted with the electrical pulse, but he did not breathe.

The EMT's prepared him for a second wave. "Clear!"

No change.

One EMT began preparing for another try, but the one on the ground held up his hand and shook his head grimly. He checked his watch. Then, he turned to Officer Smyth.

"Time of death: 10:17 pm."

Not a second sooner, Luther began coughing and slowly turned to his side. He was alive.

"He made it!" shouted the EMT. "Get a stretcher over here for him!"

Thomas rushed in and went to Luther's side as he was being lifted into the ambulance and gently touched his shoulder. "Don't worry, buddy. You'll be okay. I'll let Katrina know."

* * *

"911, what is your emergency?"

"Hello, yes. There's a robbery happening right in front of me!"

"Okay, ma'am, just stay calm. What is your location?"

"The Parkway Shop on the South End! I'm hiding in my car at one of the pumps!"

"Alright, I'm dispatching officers right now. Can you stay on the line, please? Can you describe the robbers?"

"There were four that went inside. I don't see them anymore. One of them stayed outside, and he was the lookout. He's still here — no! He's running into the store now! Oh, he's so scary looking!"

"Ma'am, could you describe him further? Why does he look scary?"

"Well, he's just so tall, and he's...black."

Monsters in Texas
Perico, Texas, 1962

"Thank you, Father."

Father Randall peered into the envelope. He thumbed over the cash in relief. They would finally be able to make a few of those small repairs they had been putting off. Utilities and food always came first for the orphanage, and many times there wasn't even enough for that.

Father Belmod shook his head, a look of regret twisting his face. "Do not thank me, Randall. This is the last of the money from me. I am afraid the Diocese has learned of our exchanges. I am being transferred."

"When?" Randall clenched the envelope in his hand, paper crinkling. Panic built in his chest. How would they survive if not from the kindness of Father Belmod? Who else would be willing to donate to the unwanted? Their orphanage stood outside of a tiny town center near the northern Texan border, too far from any city to be considered worthwhile.

"By the end of the week."

Father Belmod shifted from the tattered chair in front of the desk, using the arms to press upright. A hand went momentarily to his back as he winced. Pitiful eyes looked over the edge of wire-rimmed glasses.

Randall shifted back in his seat, running a slow hand down his face. He pushed up, leaning heavily on his worn oak desk. Any décor in the room disappeared long ago, sold off in hopes of raising money for the children.

"I will see you out, Father."

Randall sighed and forced himself to straighten, mind running frantically, trying to figure out a new source of outside funding, but coming up empty. Father Belmod nodded, a hand on the back of his chair as he waited. Randall opened the door, leading his old friend out of his study and through the barren halls. He paused before the front door.

"Thank you, Father Belmod, for all of your help. I am sorry this is the result." Sorry for them both.

Father Belmod clapped the younger man on the shoulder. "We both knew this could not last."

Randall nodded in dejection, opening the door for him. A cloud of smoke puffed into the dark, a short figure attached to a glowing point hovering beyond it. Randall cleared his throat.

The nun jumped, cigarette dangling from her fingers. "Father Belmod, Father Randall."

"Sister." Father Belmod gave her a grave nod, skirting around her and the hang of smoke in the air around her. "Best of luck, Randall."

Father Belmod returned to his car as Sister Margaret lifted the cigarette back to her lips.

"What does he mean?" she asked, exhaling smoke in Randall's direction.

Randall waved the hand still holding the crumpled envelope of cash. "We will receive nothing more from Father Belmod."

"Why?" Her lined face pulled down as she stamped out the embers of the cigarette butt.

"His actions weren't exactly sanctioned, Sister. They are moving him."

Her eyes narrowed. "Then we get it from the man who takes his place."

Father Randall sighed, shaking his head. "I doubt it will be that simple, Sister Margaret."

* * *

Sheriff Lee pulled up to the orphanage, Officer Sanchez bouncing a leg in the seat beside him. The SUV bounced across the loose gravel path, coming to a shuddering halt beside Father Randall's run-down pickup, the basket on the floor nearly toppling across Sanchez's boots. The Sheriff turned off the ignition and pulled the keys, shoving them in his pocket as they left the car, Sanchez carrying the basket.

They tromped down the well-trodden path to the front door, the cobblestones that once lined it cracked and long overgrown with weeds. The Sheriff knocked on the door.

It opened less than a second later, a tall mousy girl giving them a curious look. "Sheriff Lee, Officer Sanchez, come in. Should I get Father Randall? Sister Margaret? Sister Greta?"

"Sister Greta?" Sanchez repeated, bewildered.

Sheriff Lee shot him a look before giving the eldest orphan a soft smile. "That's okay, Linda. Let's get these muffins to breakfast."

The girl visibly brightened and opened the door wider to let them in. She led the way to the back of the orphanage, to the wide room that served as their dining area. The children sat crammed into the seats around the table, Sister Margaret standing over them. She glanced up as they came in.

"Look what they brought!"

Linda snagged the basket from Officer Sanchez, dancing her way to the table, throwing aside the towel that covered the top. Sister Margaret watched with a frown tugging down her lips but did not comment. Linda spread the goods across the table, ensuring each child got a muffin, before she collapsed into an empty space, placing the mostly empty basket on the floor beside her. Sheriff Lee watched them as they pushed aside their porridge in favor of the sugary treats. Sister Margaret crossed to the men, hands disappearing into the folds of her habit.

"Could we have a moment of your time, Sheriff?"

He frowned but nodded, surprised by the Sister addressing them.

Normally, Sister Margaret kept her eyes on the children, interacting with the police only long enough to take whatever treats they brought. She did not believe the sweets appropriate when they struggled with the basics. Yet Sheriff Lee saw no harm in giving the children a little joy.

Sister Margaret turned back to the children. "When we come back, this room should be spotless. Understand?"

The children chorused a yes, and Margaret's lips pursed, like she did not quite believe them. Even so, she led Sheriff Lee and Officer Sanchez to Father Randall's study, pausing to knock softly, not waiting for an answer before opening the door.

Father Randall stood. "Bill, David. This is a surprise. Have you met Sister Greta?"

A young woman around Officer Sanchez's age swiveled in her chair, a sweet smile lighting an angelic face. She rose easily, grace unhidden from slender limbs. She bowed her head.

"It is a pleasure to meet you."

"And you, Sister Greta. I'm Sheriff Bill Lee. This is Officer David Sanchez." He offered a hand and she hesitated, glancing at Father Randall. He inclined his head, and she took his hand cautiously, her wrist limp. James's brow furrowed. "You wanted to talk with us, Father?"

"Yes, yes, shut the door." He waited for the solid click before continuing. "We appreciate your continued generosity, Sheriff, but I am afraid the orphanage has lost our excess funding."

"What happened?" Sanchez interrupted, arms folding across a broad chest. He ignored the Sheriff's impatient look.

"Father Belmod will be leaving us. We have no guarantee of continued generosity from his replacement." Randall ran a hand through thinning brown hair. "Without that money, there is a chance we will not be able to continue to feed the eighteen children we have, let alone take in any of those newly abandoned."

Bill mimicked his officer's stance, heart dropping. "There is no solution?"

"Our best option is to put the older children, those who have been here the longest, in the foster care system."

"You can't do that!" David blurted.

Bill whirled to his unofficial partner, appalled. Father Randall appeared sympathetic.

"I am afraid we have no other choice, David. I know it is not ideal." He sank into the chair behind his desk, gesturing at the papers littering his desk, many of them stamped with red. "But I will not allow our children to starve."

The Sheriff cleared his throat. "We don't bring better news, unfortunately. Some livestock has gone missing in the area. We suspect Cartel involvement. It is unusual for them to come so far inland, but either way, you will want to keep a closer eye on the children until we figure this out."

"Thank you, Sheriff," Randall said, though he let out a groan. "Let us hope those poor animals wandered off."

Bill nodded, though he feared something much worse.

* * *

Linda tucked the last of the girls into bed, smoothing back her scraggly blonde hair. She looked around the room she shared with the other nine girls, their beds arranged in a tight maze. Her own bed sat closest to the door, threadbare blanket tucked neatly in place. Her thoughts kept her restless, though, so she passed it, flicking off the light to the room with a quick goodnight to the children within.

Linda had lived in the orphanage for ten years, long enough for her to forget any semblance of the life she had before. No one wanted the quiet mouse of a girl, with her excess freckles and frizzy brown hair. They thought her odd. Linda didn't mind, not really. She loved the other children she lived with, though her heart tinged every time one of them left her, adopted by a loving family.

That was supposed to be her. A hundred times over.

Linda crept down the stairs, skipping over the spots that creaked. It was past curfew. Should Sister Margaret find her, she'd get a scolding like no other, forced to clean every crevice with a toothbrush. So she avoided the front door, where the Sister likely stood smoking, as if no one knew of her habit. She could try to cover it with that horrid rose water all she liked, but the smoke lingered and stained.

Skirting Father Randall's study, Linda made her way to the kitchen. Froze. Her eyes blinked rapidly.

"Linda?" The new Sister sat on a stool; hands cupped around a steaming cup. "You should be in bed."

The gears of her mind worked in a fervor, desperately trying to come up with a decent excuse. She had forgotten about Sister Greta. Linda didn't know her schedule yet, her habits.

"Sorry, Sister Greta. I didn't mean to bother you. I was supposed to go get more water from the well out back for our washing tomorrow, but I'm afraid I forgot," she said, casting her eyes down like she was embarrassed to be caught slacking. Their plumbing was rudimentary at best, and the orphans gathered water every day for washing of dishes and bodies. Hopefully, the Sister didn't realize someone already took care of the water for the baths tomorrow.

Sister Greta gave her a stern look, odd on her young face. "Very well. Be quick, Linda."

Linda nodded, grabbing the two buckets by the door before heading outside. Not exactly how she wanted to spend her time outside, but it got her out, let the night air soothe the ragged edges of her mind.

She overheard their plan when she went to give back the basket. Overheard Father Randall saying they would go into the system, Officer Sanchez protesting as if it was the worst thing in the world.

Linda would be the first to go. She knew it. She was the oldest child here by three years, and the majority of the children were under nine. She didn't know much about the foster care system, but for Officer Sanchez to dislike it, for Father Randall to save it as a last resort…

Linda didn't think it would be a pleasant experience.

Wind whipping through her hair, Linda wound her way through their tiny garden to the old stone well at the edge of the property, near the woods. She sat the buckets near the base and moved to the handle.

She yelped. A pair of feet poked out from around the side, covered with muddy boots. Linda took slow, tentative steps, waiting for the eldest of the boys to jump out at her. The feet didn't move, though, heavy gasps too low to be any of the boys, the lack of robes saying it wasn't Father Randall.

"Officer Sanchez?" she asked, rounding the well. "Sheriff Lee?"

The man let out a low moan, not answering.

Linda crouched in the dark, the shadowy face unfamiliar. She put a hand on his arm. Yanked immediately away, hand coming away wet and sticky. Linda held it up to the dim moonlight. Her heart let out an unsteady thud of disbelief. Blood.

"Sir?"

She shook his shoulder, hoping she found a dry patch. He roused momentarily but slumped back down. Linda shook him again. He moaned.

"You…danger…" he croaked.

Linda cast a frantic glance over her shoulder, back to the orphanage. She should get Sister Greta. But the Sister would likely send her away, not allow her to learn why this man was here, who he was. If Linda brought him inside…. She would already be involved.

"Come on."

She grunted, trying to haul his arm—the non-bloody one—over her shoulder. Linda managed to get him seated but no further. He was too big. Too heavy.

She slumped to the ground. "Come on," she pleaded. "I need you to help me."

The man beside her groaned, and to her surprise, shifted. With her help, he stood, leaning heavily on her, the weight heavier than any buckets she had ever carried. They limped back to the orphanage together. Linda struggled with every step, listening to the ragged breaths of the man beside her.

Minutes morphed to hours, the trip back to the kitchen door took too long. She leaned the man against the siding near the door so she could reach the handle, twisting, and shoving the door open with her foot.

"Linda! What are you doing?"

"Help," she begged Sister Greta, revealing the figure twice her size still on her shoulder.

"What…" Sister Greta's eyes flew wide at the sight before her, irises flicking over the lolling head, the bloody slash, the dragging feet. She sprang to put her mug on the counter near the wall, clearing the prep table with a careless swipe of her hand. "Give me his arms, Linda. Take his feet."

Together they hauled the man onto the table, his back scraping as they grappled with his body. His head rolled to the side, eyes opened in mere slits, his mouth hanging open.

"Is he…?"

"No." Sister Greta ran assessing eyes over the figure once more. She rushed to the phone mounted on the wall, punching in three numbers. The phone pulled away from her ear, and she stared at it, hit the receiver, tried again. "The lines are down. Water, Linda. We need clean water, fresh rags, and the first aid kit. Quickly."

Linda didn't question, not with the frantic sternness coloring the Sister's normally soft voice. She rushed back outside, back and shoulder aching, and drew water from the well faster than she ever had before, water splashing as she dumped it from the tied bucket to the larger buckets at the base. Her carelessness and haste left her boots soaked, the old soles leaking water into her socks.

Ignoring the squelching of wet shoes on dirt, she lugged the sloshing buckets back to the kitchen, rummaging through cabinets and finding their largest pot. The stove turned on with a hiss and a click, blue fire springing to life beneath the pot. She dumped the first bucket in and hastened to their laundry room, grabbing the rags they normally used for cleaning. Linda tossed them over her shoulder, and rushed to the bathroom, taking the bulky first aid kit from beneath the sink.

By the time she returned, the man's chest and bloodied arm laid bare, camouflaged uniform cut away to puddle around him. If his pale skin didn't lay bloody and bruised, red overlapping with deep purple, Linda may have blushed. She had seen the bare chests of the boys in the orphanage—there was a lake nearby they visited sometimes in the heat of summer. But boys' scrawny chests were nothing like the man on the table, chiseled muscles clear beneath the swaths of injury.

Linda gagged at the sight of the full extent of his wounds, edging closer, one arm cast over her nose from the putrid copper scent. Red oozed from three jagged slashes from bicep to the opposite side of the ribcage. Short tears and scratches overlapped with bruises. Sister Greta lifted her eyes to meet Linda's.

"Check the water, Linda. We need it to boil then cool enough to wash away the blood. Do you have a sewing kit? With embroidery floss?"

Linda bit her lip. Shook her head. "I don't know what that is."

She had needle and thread, since the girls were in charge of darning any rips and holes in clothes, but what was embroidery floss?

Sister Greta let out a groan and immediately covered her mouth. "I am sorry, Linda. Get your needle and the regular thread. We will have to double it over to be thick enough."

Linda ran out once more, returning with her needle and multiple spools of thread. Sister Greta leaned over the man with a measuring cup of water hot enough to steam the sides. With a grimace, she dumped it across his wounds, dark red washing pink down his sides.

"The iodine from the kit, Linda, with a rag. Quickly."

Linda nodded, tearing open the first aid bag and finding the glass bottle. She handed the rag and bottle over to Sister Greta. The man hissed as the iodine hit his wounds, eyes scrunched tight. The wound didn't appear to be bleeding anymore, though, the ragged edges of skin revealing deep pink tissue beneath and a peek of ivory. Bone. Linda couldn't it stop the bile this time and upchucked into the sink.

"Breathe, Linda, in through your nose, out through your mouth. Drink some water. I'll need your help with stitching."

Linda puked one more time for good measure and rinsed out her mouth with water before returning to Sister Greta's side.

"You will need to hold him down while I stitch, understand." Sister Greta showed her where to hold, and Linda nodded, relieved she didn't have to do the actual stitching. She grabbed his wrists, leaning over the table for leverage. And Sister Greta pierced his skin.

He yelped, jerking, and Linda nearly lost her grip. She gritted her teeth and gripped harder. His eyes flew wide, head frantic in its movement.

"Stay still. This wound is deep," Sister Greta instructed.

"I… I have to…" He tilted his chin down, observing the quick slip of the needle, and groaned, stilling with apparent understanding. "My bag. Where is my bag?"

"What bag?" Sister Greta asked calmly while Linda's brow knitted in confusion. She didn't remember seeing a bag, but that didn't mean it hadn't been out there, tucked away in the darkness.

"My bag… with… ammo…." he gasped, just as Father Randall burst into the kitchen.

"What is going on?" he demanded at the sight before him. "Who is this man?"

"James, sir." He coughed and winced as Sister Greta's needle dug into him once more. "James Forrester, with the 10th Special Forces Group." His eyes squeezed shut, like the string of words took too much out of him. "I'm afraid you're all in terrible danger."

With that, he went limp. Sister Greta paused, glancing up at Father Randall. "I'm sorry, Father. I tried to call for the ambulance, but the lines are dead. I didn't want to disturb you."

Father Randall rubbed his face. "The next time someone is bleeding out on our doorstep, Sister Greta, please fetch me at once." He turned a stern gaze on Linda. "What are you doing out of bed?"

"Sorry, Father, I—"

"No." He waved away whatever excuse she had been about to give him. "You will return to bed at once."

"But, Father, Sister Greta—"

"Has my help now. Go on, Linda."

A pout formed on Linda's lips, and she stalked towards the hall, pausing in the doorway. "I found him leaning on the well. His bag is probably there too."

Father Randall sighed. "Goodnight, Linda."

Her shoulders slumped. "Goodnight, Father. Sister." *James.*

* * *

A high-pitched whir dragged James from sleep. He bolted upright from the bed in the boys' shared room. *No. It has to be a dream.*

The noise continued, followed by a low clacking and the buzz of wings.

Not a dream.

James bolted from bed, slinging on his uniform pants and lacing up his boots.

"James?" The oldest boy, Tommy, rubbed his eyes, sitting up slowly in his bed across the room.

James threw on his spare jacket from his bag—the original uniform was in tatters and trashed, and did up the buttons, tossing his bag over the shoulder.

"Get up, Tommy. Get the other boys. Close the shutters. Lock the door." James tucked his pistol at his hip, checked his rifle. Tommy's eyes widened. "Don't come out, no matter what you hear. Do you understand?"

Tommy's head bobbed, and James added his knife to his belt, just in case. The whir grew louder, clacks banging through his skull. With a scowl, James left the boys, banging on the door to the room the Sisters shared.

"Sisters!" he shouted in case his knock didn't rouse them. "Get up, go to the girls. It's happening."

Not waiting for a response, he went further down the hall, waking Father Randall. "Father, get to the boys."

He would not risk them if he did not have to. It didn't sound like a group of them. Likely a scout, sent ahead to follow his scent. James gritted his teeth. One. Just one of them. Not the ten that tore his unit to shreds, not the ten that feasted on the bones of his friends as they ran and hid, injured, until they left. He thought they hadn't noticed. He thought he would have a few more days. His stitches pulled at his arm. They would be ripped before the end of the night.

James took the steps two at a time. He had twenty bullets in his M14, seven in his Colt Government. If it took more than that….

It's just a scout, he reassured himself.

Heart hammering in his chest, he rounded the bottom of the stairs when a *boom* racked the walls. He rushed to the back door as another *boom* shook the floor. It wasn't giving up its lost prey.

James considered his options, brain whirling. Open the door, turn the table, shoot from his barricade? No, that gave it the opportunity to slip inside or break its way in. There wasn't a window he could get vantage from, not in the square-shaped building, not while it slammed against the back door, desperate to find him.

There was only one option.

James turned the other way, rushing through the halls and carefully opening the front door, hand at his hip, ready to pull his pistol should any of the creatures await him, the banging a distraction.

Nothing, merely empty darkness. His back to the wall, James skirted the building just as glass shattered. A sharp cry followed, and the attack on the building ceased, while James's eyes flew wide. *No.*

He rushed around the building, following the whimper, his feet sure. He pulled the rifle from his back, fitted it neatly on his shoulder. Paused at the corner to the back. His heart sank at the sound of wet clicking, the whir shifting to a near purr. He knew that sound. That sound haunted his nightmares.

He rounded the corner, taking the split second to identify his distracted target, the weak spots between the carapace, and fired. Bullet, after bullet, after bullet.

Until it splatted.

James approached cautiously, taking in the glittering green-black of its three sectioned body, the ends of shining wings that were now ripped and bloodied, the antenna that still twitched. A boy's lifeless eyes stared up at the moon, crushed beneath the massive insect-like thing. James turned his head, not willing to look and see who it could be, though the cold wrapping his heart knew.

He shoved the carapace off the boy with his foot just as Father Randall appeared at the dented kitchen door, mouth agape. The priest crossed himself, muttering prayers under his breath as he hastily shut the door as quickly as it opened. James paid him no mind. Blamed his retreat not at all. He would retreat too, if he could.

This was the first time James got the chance to examine one up close. The body itself stood at least seven feet tall, the odd stick-like legs with needle-sharp hairs bringing it easily to ten, should it stand. It's black globe-like eyes were empty now, but James knew they glowed red when alive.

The torso folded across itself into a million little ridges, like it somehow became clothed in armor better than any bulletproof vest. His squad learned that the hard way, shooting for the heart only for the bullets to ricochet. The only places to aim were into the eye itself or where each part of the torso connected. Which, when the target could fly, became difficult even for a qualified sniper.

James took a deep breath. Turned from the alien or experiment gone wrong or whatever the grotesque insect was. He knelt by the boy, unable to throw up the wall around his heart in time. Tommy. He must have followed James, the soldier too engrossed in the task at hand to hear him. James kept his eyes on his innocent face, the only place on his body not drenched in blood. He had been too late to stop the thing from feasting.

With a flick of his fingers, James closed the boy's eyes and shoved to his feet. He tromped to the door, shoving it open and sinking against the nearby counter. *One… two… three… four… five….*

He straightened. Father Randall stared at him, his mouth working soundlessly.

"I need a shovel," James said.

Father Randall nodded, head heavy. "I will help you."

James shook his head, not meeting the Father's eyes as he said, "I can't let you do that, Father. This is my fault. My responsibility."

"What is that thing?" Father Randall asked after he fetched a shovel from the nearest closet.

"I don't know. But I do know there's a chance it's not the last."

Father Randall collapsed onto a stool. "I will call the Sheriff in the morning."

James took the shovel but didn't comment. Whatever they did, they needed to do it soon.

Or Tommy wouldn't be the last casualty.

* * *

A sharp knock reverberated through the downstairs. A bleary-eyed James opened the front door, one hand wrapped around a mug of too-strong coffee. The two men outside sized him up, the Sheriff's hand going to rest on the pistol at his hip, James's own pistol still hidden by the door. He blinked at them, taking in the shining badges attached to their chest.

"He's already here, Father!" James called over his shoulder, opening the door wider and beckoning the men inside. "I'm James Forrester."

He stuck out a hand and immediately grimaced, his stitches pulling. Between shooting his rifle and digging two shallow graves, he was lucky he hadn't ripped open the wound despite Sister Greta's neat tending.

The Sheriff took his hand after a moment's hesitation. "I'm Sheriff Bill Lee."

Officer Sanchez introduced himself as well, before both men set off for the Father's study, Sanchez holding tight to a box stained with grease.

"Father Randall?" Bill prompted once inside the office.

Randall grimaced. "You need to see this, Bill." He paused from pushing up in his chair, noticing the box in Sanchez's hand. "You can go give that to the kids, David."

Sanchez nodded and ducked out. Bill frowned. "See what, Father?"

Father Randall shook his head, gesturing for him to follow. James led the way outside, to the massive grave he dug near the kitchen. The body was too big for anyone to carry, even with help. He hadn't yet covered it, though Tommy's body was already covered in a patch of fresh earth, far from the creature.

"Holy Mother of God," the Sheriff gasped. "What is that?"

"An abomination," Father Randall concurred, not bothering to chide him on his choice of words. "A spawn of the Devil."

James wisely kept his thoughts to himself. This was no creation of God. Man-made or alien, there was no chance God, or Satan, concocted such a creature.

"A pack of them took out my squad near the border," James informed the Sheriff, just as Officer Sanchez strolled out to meet them.

"*Ay Dios mío.*" The man crossed himself, eyes wide.

"They're monstrous but killable if you aim for the right spot," James continued. He pointed to each weak spot on the body. "This will not be the last of 'em."

"The livestock." Bill's mouth twisted at the realization.

"Could be a food source, yes," James told him.

Sanchez looked at him, frantic. "You think they will return?"

"They tracked me here once; they'll likely do it again. Especially if their scout doesn't return. They can follow its scent too."

Sheriff Lee folded his arms. "How much time do we have?"

"It took a day for it to track me here. If we're lucky, we've got a few more hours."

"We must evacuate," Father Randall insisted, something he had touched on with James the night before. "We must get the children somewhere safe."

"We'll take them to the police station," Sheriff Lee said. He fished his keys out of his pockets and tossed them to Officer Sanchez. "Take the youngest five with you, David. Send back up this way, guns at the ready. Father Randall here can pile the other youngins in his truck and follow."

Father Randall shook his head. "Take the five, David, like the Sheriff said, but there are things we must pack. Once we do that, I'll follow."

"Tell 'em it's a field trip and they'll have to take turns," James interjected. "We don't need 'em panicking."

David appeared like he was going to argue but thought better of it, rushing back inside with the keys in his hand, giving the monster one last glance. A shudder ran down his spine as he disappeared inside.

"I'm going to cover it up, hope that buys us some more time. Sheriff, my bag of ammunitions is upstairs beneath my bed. I got another rifle you can take and a few pistols for the Father and Sisters, plus a few knives. Everyone should have a gun and a knife."

Bill shook his head. "Giving untrained civilians guns is dangerous."

"So is leavin' 'em unarmed." James gave him a hard look. "They're the best chance this place has got right now."

The Sheriff considered the younger soldier, pressing back memories that threatened to swell at the talk of guns and best chances. He dipped his chin. And hoped they weren't all making a big mistake.

* * *

The orphanage turned upside down. Tables and beds shoved on their sides and barricaded windows. Chairs stacked in a tower, ready to block doorways. Adults armed with guns and hunting knives and kitchen knives. Linda wanting to join in the fight and being refused, over and over again. They would be evacuating soon, they promised her. There was no need for her to fight. They would be out of here before anything happened.

Lies.

Whirs overlapped clacks and melded with a sharp whistling sound, and James shut his eyes in a moment of silent prayer.

"They're here, and there's more than one!" he shouted.

"Go, children, go!"

The kids, eating lunch in a moment of peace, fled, plates and food flying as they bolted in terror. James maneuvered to the back window, looking through with his heart thumping in his ears. The Sheriff shifted into the space beside him, his rifle at the ready.

"How many?"

"Four."

"Father Randall, Sister Greta!" Bill barked. "Upstairs. Guard the children. Sister Margaret, get the front door, guard our flank."

James's eyes slid to him for a brief second. "Soldier?"

"Korean War." Bill jerked his chin in a nod. "Thought my fighting days were over."

James clapped him on the shoulder. "Glad you have my back, Sheriff."

"You ready?"

James grunted his response, and together they edged to the door, backs pressed to the wall. If they played this right, they could kill all four without casualties. There was still time before they reached the orphanage. With quick, sharply placed shots, they could win this.

"Now!"

The Sheriff threw open the door. James moved to follow him out. Nearly ran into his back.

"I thought you said there were four."

"There were."

Bill stepped aside to reveal three, diving straight for them. James swore there were four seconds ago. It didn't matter. No time to think. To worry. James lifted his rifle.

Sister Margaret stumbled back as the front door splintered and the work of Satan broke through.

She brandished the pistol with both hands, shoulders shuddering. She pulled shot after shot. Tried to aim for the places James told her. Watched as her bullets went into the walls. Bounced off the shining black monster and buried into the floor.

Margaret scrambled up the stairs. Pulled the trigger as the thing hovered in the doorway, orb-like eyes of hell trained on her. The gun clicked. Empty. Every bullet wasted.

She pulled the kitchen knife. Her pulse throbbed angrily in her throat. Her body washed cold. Margaret knew what came next. Knew her fate as the thing buzzed towards her, pincers ready to devour.

Margaret lifted the knife in defiance, every bone in her body screaming at her to run. Her children were upstairs. If she did not kill it, they would surely die.

Gathering her courage, Sister Margaret let out a final yell and lunged towards death.

Sister Greta let out a scream.

An insect-creature burst through the window at the end of the hall, talons clacking. She backed into Father Randall, desperate to distance herself from the impossible. The Father put a hand on her shoulder, gave her a brief squeeze, and lifted his pistol.

Greta stepped to the side. Lifted her own gun with trembling hands. She had faced monsters. Lived with one her whole life until she fled to the church. *Just another bully*, she told herself. *Just another massive, angry, drunk, set on beating you within an inch of your life.*

Not this time.

Together they aimed, Sister Greta aiming for the eyes, the red globes the perfect bright target. Father Randall aimed low, for the skinny part of the carapace. A supposed weak spot. Her shots go wide. Glance off its head. Hit the antenna. It lets out a high-pitched careening wail, pincers stretching, ready to kill.

Father Randall muttered a Hail Mary beneath his breath. Eyes squeezing shut, Sister Greta sent a prayer to God.

And fired.

A massive body dropped to the ground in a crash, the building shaking. Bill and James paid it no mind, their rifles spent, pistols aiming.

A shadow flashed over them, bigger than the rest, letting out a low noise that vibrated their very bones. It shrieked. Both of them clapped hands over their ears, their bodies seizing, vision blurring. The shadow dove. Bill scrambled back. Too late. The pincers wrapped around his outstretched leg. James stretched for his dropped pistol; his fingers unable to grasp the grip.

The big one took off, leg in hand, dripping blood in massive splotches. Crimson splashed over Bill's face. Wet James's back.

The two they were facing followed with an angry buzz, leaving them trembling.

James waited, shakes slowly subsiding, and ensured the insects were mere specks in the sky when he bent next to Bill. He frowned at his ragged pantleg, cut at the middle of the calf. No blood.

"What…?"

Bill wiped his face with his sleeve. "Prosthetic. Lost that lower half in the war."

James let out a low whistle, helping Bill to his feet. Foot. "Luck's with you today."

"With all of us, I would say. One dead. The big one had a knife in its eye. Saw it before it bled all over me." Bill ran the hem of his uniform across his eyes. "And they retreated. We need to get out of here before they come back. Make sure David's okay. It doesn't take that long to get to the police station and back. Backup should've been here by now."

James dragged Bill back inside, fearing the worst.

* * *

Sister Margaret was dead. Along with two boys found huddled around the corner from the Sister, like they tried to escape only to find their path blocked.

Father Randall wanted to bury them.

James argued there was no time. The Sheriff agreed. Instead they put them in a barricaded room, sheets covering their bodies, until they could give them a proper burial. If they ever got that chance.

The remaining children piled into the bed of Father Randall's truck, James squeezing in with them with a reloaded rifle. Between hasty packing and washing off blood, the sky turned to hint at dusk. Darkness would fall soon after, and James had a sinking suspicion the things would return in hopes of catching them unawares.

Each child cradled their small bag in their laps, fear turning them silent. They held onto one another, heads on each other's shoulders, fingers laced together. The touch brought the comfort they so desperately needed.

James kept an eye to the sky as they drove, one hand on his rifle, the other on the end of the bed, waiting. Watching.

And nearly tumbling out as the truck came to a screeching halt. Dirt kicked up in their wake, their pull to the side of the road too quick.

James stood as the doors slammed, jumping down to the ground with a wince. He needed to be careful. He was still healing. *Once this is over*, he promised himself. *I'll rest when it's over.*

James stalked to the front. "Father? What is it?"

Father Randall only shook his head, a puddle of vomit by his boots. James rounded the side and gagged.

The Sheriff's SUV stood overturned in the ditch, metal dented, glass shattered, the pile of red and white indiscernible next to it, except for the glint of bronze that shone on top.

Officer Sanchez died protecting them. James swallowed bile. The insects did not care, eating through his body to feast on the children below. Five children. The youngest among the orphans. Gone. Because they tried to save them.

James let a moment of silence pass before he spoke. In respect to the children and to ensure his own pile of puke didn't join the Father's. "We have to keep going. It's too late. I'm sorry."

Father Randall nodded numbly but made no move. James steered him back to the passenger's side, eyes meeting Sister Greta's.

"You'll need to drive."

Her usually soft face set in a hard line, tears trailing down a clenched jaw. She scooted into the driver's seat, and Bill moved to allow Father Randall into his spot.

They drove in silence for ten more minutes when Father Randall's truck sputtered and smoked. Stalled. It came to a shaking halt.

"Two miles to the station," the Sheriff called out. "We can walk." He paused. "Well. You can walk. I need some help."

"Father Randall, help the Sheriff, take the front. Sister Greta, gather the children. I'll take the rear."

They marched in an odd clump down the road, sticking to the dusty sides in case a car barreled past. None did. With the Sheriff's slowed pace, it took them nearly two hours, and they stumbled into the station as darkness fully descended on them.

No one was there.

* * *

Sheriff Lee tried to call his deputies' homes. James wasn't surprised to learn the lines were dead. He tried the radios next, yet they gave him static, crinkling in their ears, murmuring *helpless*. James refused to give up though and asked Bill if the station had a ham radio. The Sheriff gave him a shrug of defeat, told him to check their storage rooms.

Some luck lingered. James found one and set about turning it on. It whirred to life, and James set the proper knobs to what he hoped were the right channels.

"This is Sergeant James Forrester, Bravo Company, Second Battalion, 10th Special Forces Group," he called into the mouthpiece. "SOS. This is Sergeant James Forrester."

The line crackled. James held his breath. *Please.*

"Report, Sergeant," came the staticky response a too-long moment later.

A wave of relief washed over him. He gave them an update about it all. His squad. The orphanage. The monsters. He waited for them to express disbelief, to tell him he was crazy.

"Location, Sergeant."

James sagged. "One moment, Sir." He dropped the mouthpiece and leaned out the door. "What's the address, Sheriff?" The Sheriff called back almost immediately, sounding distracted, and James relayed it back to whoever was on the other line.

"ETA three hours, Sergeant. Hunker down. Help is on the way."

"Thank you, Sir," James nearly cried into the microphone. "Thank you."

He disconnected. James took a moment, breathing through the utter hope lighting his chest, when something rapped. He jumped then chided himself. These monsters didn't knock.

The front door was already open when he made his way out of the back room. The group stumbled their way in, holding each other up, bloody and broken. *Survivors.*

Father Randall and Sister Greta rushed to pull chairs from desks to allow them to gather together, clearing desks to lie those worse off onto a flat surface. An elderly man limped towards Father Randall, his robes disheveled, wire-rim glasses askew.

"Father Randall," he gasped.

Randall rushed forward as the older man collapsed, grasping him by the shoulders. He settled the man into the nearest seat and crouched in front of him. Concern etched his features. "Father Belmod. What happened?"

The old man only shook his head, face crumpled. Another spoke for him, looking a little less for wear than the others, the splatter of blood on his cheek not his own.

"We're the only ones left." The man's voice came out hoarse. From disbelief, or from screaming, James did not know. "Those *things* came out of nowhere. We couldn't fight them. Bullets didn't touch them." His mouth pressed in a firm line. "They broke through our doors, our windows." He shook his head, eyes glassy. "I doubt there's anyone else."

James made a slow count of the people in the room. Twenty survivors from the town at most, many of them around his age, Father Belmod the lone elder amongst them. How had the old man made it?

"Help is coming," James told them. "But it's a few hours out. Those monsters will come back. Sister Greta can tend to the wounded. Have some of the older children help. Those who're able will arm themselves. Bullets do hurt 'em. You just gotta find the right place to shoot. The eyes is best. But the skinny part in between their big ends is good too. If you're too injured to fight, then you'll go with the children. Where's the safest place, Sheriff?"

"The back room, most likely. No windows, no outside doors."

James grimaced, safe, maybe, but they'd be on top of one another. "Did anyone come armed?"

The man who spoke for Father Belmod raised his hand, along with a few more. Six left to arm, if James guessed correctly about their injuries.

"Sheriff, you have an armory?"

Bill pointed to a door near the back room. James nodded, hoping they had more than just a few police-issued pistols waiting out there.

"Let's get to work."

Linda watched as James passed out the guns he found, instructing them on loading and firing as quickly as he could. She didn't want to be stuck with Sister Greta, wiping down blood and bandaging wounds. She truly wanted to help. To defend the others. The kids she considered siblings. The people she cared for the most.

Linda didn't know these strangers from the town. She didn't *care* about them. She didn't want them to die, but Sister Greta could manage. Their injuries weren't that bad. They never would've made it to the police station if they were.

A light buzzing filled her ears. Her heart dropped, eyes immediately finding James. He glanced to the ceiling. Scowled. She watched him pull his courage on like a jacket before he checked his guns, his knife.

"They're coming. Fast." The buzzes turned to whirs as the things approached, still only specks on the horizon. "Everyone, find a window, a door. Do *not* let 'em in. We just gotta hold off until help arrives. An hour. We can do it. Sister Greta, take the kids."

Linda didn't follow at first, adrenaline pumping. Father Randall gave her a hard look. "Linda!"

"Helping the injured, Father," she insisted. Anything to keep her in the action a second longer.

Sheriff Lee held out a hand expectantly to James. "Give me a rifle, kid."

"Bill, you can't stand!" exclaimed Father Randall before James could respond.

Linda hooked her arm around Father Belmod, escorting him with measured paces to the back room.

"I can sit and shoot, and I'm one of the few that's trained. Give me the damn rifle!"

James silently went back to get another rifle while Father Randall shook his head. "You're going to get yourself killed, Bill."

Bill set his jaw as Linda handed Father Belmod over to Sister Greta, returning to help Sheriff Lee.

"Put the chair there, Linda," he said, pointing to the spot right in front of the main doors. "So be it, Father. I would rather die fighting for these people than cower like a yellow-bellied coward."

Linda plopped the chair facing the doors, clacking joining the whirs. She could see bodies now, massive wasp-like things but black, swarming ever closer.

She gulped. Trying to mask the edge of fear, she helped the Sheriff situate himself in the chair, his stump of a leg outstretched awkwardly in front of him. James handed him a rifle and clapped him on the shoulder, dipping his chin. He didn't speak, though, backing away with his own rifle raised, eyes on the windows.

Linda froze. Clacks and whirs and whines threatened to break her eardrums, a thousand times worse than she had heard at the orphanage. She clamped her hands over her ears as her mind swam, eyes squeezing shut. What *was* that?

"Linda!" James shouted over the din. Linda forced her eyes back open, horror sinking into her bones at the terror etched on the soldier's normally careful face. "Get to the back room. Go!"

Palms pressed tightly over her ears, Linda listened. James's fear spurred her forward, reaching the back room as the sound increased. The sound dropped her to her knees. Hands grabbed at her, yanking her into the room and slamming the door.

James's heart threatened to beat right out of his chest. He took quick breaths at the sight before them. Not one, or three, or ten. But hundreds. Hundreds of monsters with wicked red eyes, a cloud of them. He could only watch as they bolted past the windows, the horrid jolting whirs and clacks coming from everywhere, threatening to consume him.

We just have to make it an hour. Just until help arrives. The words were no comfort. He pressed back tears. He knew where this would lead if just one of those monsters managed to break through into the station.

James didn't let himself think of home as he raised his rifle, yelling out what he hoped sounded courageous, inspiring.

"We will not yield!"

Fire and Rain

Dust flew as a convoy of U.S. Army Humvees rolled through the desert. It was their usual patrol route. PFC James Young sat in the back of the vehicle that was bringing up the rear. He wiped the sweat from his eyes and leaned his head forward to avoid bumping his Kevlar helmet on the inside of the vehicle as they bounced along on the uneven terrain. The Middle East was hot, hot in a way that constantly surprised him. Even the hottest summer in the US wouldn't be this bad. Thirty minutes in the dry air made your throat feel like it was about to crack into a thousand pieces.

This was James' third tour while on active duty. He had always dreamed of being in the military since his dad and grandfather were military men themselves – his grandfather in the Air Force and his father in the Army. While his tours had never been a walk in the park by any means, he thanked his lucky stars that he had escaped any brushes with imminent death. After this tour, it would also be the end of his contract, and he decided he would hang up his fatigues in pursuit of civilian life.

Sitting next to James in the backseat was his buddy, Johnny. Years ago, they had gone through Basic together and now found themselves in the same platoon. Johnny was a family man, with a wife and kid back home, and had been pestering James to settle down with a good woman. Johnny caught his eye and gave him a lopsided grin.

"You making lovey-dovey eyes at me isn't gonna get me in your tent tonight, Young," he teased.

James rolled his eyes but went along with Johnny's antics. "Enough time in this desert makes me a desperate man. There's no way you'll reconsider?"

Johnny held up his hands. "Katie would kill me if she ever found out. It's the wife's rules, not mine. You know I think you're a fine specimen."

James snorted and shook his head. "How are they doing, by the way?"

"Katie and Luke? Aw, they're great, man. The best family a guy could ask for." He pulled a laminated photo out of his pocket – a picture of Luke, his son.

Johnny tapped the photo with a dusty finger. "Luke turns seven years old next month; can you believe that? His birthday is the day before we get home. Happy Birthday to him, right?" he grinned. "I convinced Katie to wait to have the party until after I get back since I haven't been to my own son's birthday party in years. Think the last one was when he turned three."

James shook his head. "At least you've got this one, my friend. He's going to love it, too."

Johnny grinned, and James could see a slight mist in his eyes. Johnny cleared his throat and asked, "So what about you and Suzie? How's your gal doing back home?"

Suzie Oswald was James' childhood sweetheart. Over the years, while James was stateside, they had...gotten to know each other as adults. They had been writing letters back and forth for the last few months, and though he would never admit it to his buddies, James was madly in love. He was set on asking her to marry him when he returned home – even though he knew that Suzie's well-to-do parents would have much to say on that matter.

James sighed with a smile on his face. "She's good, man. Real good. I think, uh...I think I might pop the big question when I get home."

"Ha! No shit?" Johnny reached over and slapped James on the knee with a grin. "That's fantastic! I was beginning to wonder what was going on with all the letters I've seen coming to you since we got here – more than she sent you in Basic. She's crazy about you, man. Oh, and those drawings she sends you? Whew! Your girl's got some talent."

James nodded proudly. "She's an artist. Well, on the side, anyway." He paused as their vehicle hit a large bump in the road. "She's an accountant, for now – thanks to her stuffy parents – but she's really trying to make her art a full-time thing."

"Shoot, I tell you, Young, she's a hell of a woman.Just like my Katie. Oh, Lord!" Johnny looked up to the ceiling with a wide grin. "Sometimes you just miss them so much feels like your chest is gonna explode, doesn't it? Man, I just want to get out of this dust bowl and see my son. Go to his birthday party. Play catch in the yard. Talk to him about anything and everything. When we get home, I'm gonna—"

BOOM!

"Contact right!" shouted someone.

An enormous explosion suddenly rocked their vehicle! The driver slammed on the brakes, and men began piling out of the convoy. James' stomach twisted as he flung himself out of the vehicle, rifle at the ready.

Outside the Humvee, chaos was quickly taking over: men shouting and screaming, the sound of rapid gunfire, the smoky smell of something burning in the air. James looked ahead and almost vomited. Their lead vehicle had hit an IED – that's where the burning smell was coming from. The Humvee was completely destroyed, and the outlines of the soldiers that had been inside could be faintly seen through the flames that engulfed the remains.

James snapped back into reality as a bullet whizzed past his head. He hugged the side of his Humvee and slid along its edge, peeking over the hood. He could see an ambush group on the ridge up to their right. The other soldiers of the convoy had spotted them as well, and they fanned out in battle formation using the Humvees as cover. Johnny knelt to James' right, firing shots from behind the trunk of the vehicle. James raised his rifle to his shoulder and peered down the sights. *Pop, pop, pop!* He picked off three of the attackers. He paused to take a deep breath then focused down the sights once more. *Pop, pop, pop!* Only two that time, but the remaining attackers began to fall back. They had not anticipated such a heavy response, and now they fled into the hills in retreat.

The gunfire dwindled down then stopped altogether. James cautiously eased himself forward, scanning the ridge for any more signs of danger. The other soldiers began to emerge as well, not one of them let their guard down.

James let out a breath and shook his head. "Johnny, we've got to clear the rest of this area and check for wounded. Johnny?" He turned and stopped short. His eyes grew wide, and his pulse quickened once more.

Johnny stood, frozen in place, pointing his rifle behind the Humvee. Facing him was a young boy. The boy couldn't have been more than eight years old. His clothes were dirty and ragged. His face was twisted into a scowl, but tracks of tears cut through the dust on his cheeks. In his small, shaking hands, he clutched an AK-47 rifle – and it was pointed right at Johnny.

James swallowed hard and slowly started walking towards Johnny and the boy, but Johnny held up his hand to signal a stop. James heard rumors that they had been sending children to the front lines, but this was the first time his unit had ever seen one. Without taking his eyes off the young kid, Johnny raised both his hands in the air, still holding his own gun.

Johnny began to speak softly, "Hey, little buddy. It's alright. I'm not gonna hurt you. I am a friend, not an enemy." He took a step closer, but the boy tightened his grip on his rifle with a whimper.

"Alright, that's cool." Johnny stopped. "You remind me of my boy at home. His name is Luke. What's your name?"

The boy trembled but never lowered the barrel of his gun.

"Okay, okay." Johnny tossed his rifle to the side.

"What the hell are you doing?" James hissed in a panic.

"Calm down, Young. There's no way in hell I'm taking him down, so I've got to get him to trust me. He's just a kid." Johnny stepped forward again with his empty hands in the air. "Alright, little man, I don't have anything now. It's just you and me. I dropped mine. Now you can drop yours." He waved his hands, motioning for the child to drop his own weapon.

The boy shook and took a step backward but didn't move his gun.

Johnny cautiously took another step forward and smiled warmly. "It's okay; you can trust me. Just drop the gun, little man. It's all going to be—"

BANG!

Johnny's head snapped back, and his body crumpled to the ground. The little boy stood, pale and frozen as he finally lowered the smoking barrel of his rifle.

James heard a scream that sounded much like his own, but he couldn't feel himself screaming. He couldn't feel his feet running forward. He couldn't feel anything. It was like he was watching a movie, completely separated from his body.

He watched as his arms raised his rifle to his shoulder. He watched as he looked down the barrel. He watched as the little boy's head came into view, right between his sights.

James squeezed his eyes shut tight and pulled the trigger.

Eight weeks later

James took a long sip of his coffee and frowned. He had made the cup of Irish coffee a little too Irish, even for his taste. He picked up the bottle of whiskey that sat next to the coffee maker and gazed at it as if blaming it for jumping into his coffee itself.

This was James' second week home in Myrtle Beach, South Carolina since his tour. And things weren't exactly going well. James had been suffering from vivid nightmares, so he hadn't slept well in weeks. He was haunted by the memory of his friend, Johnny, and he blamed himself for Johnny's death. Every time he closed his eyes, he saw Johnny's head snapping back and the boy who had shot him. He saw the boy in the sights of his rifle and felt himself pulling the trigger...

"AUGH!" James yelled and hurled the bottle of whiskey against the wall behind him, shattering it into a million pieces. Liquor splattered everywhere. He pounded his fists on the counter and kicked the cabinets, with a red-hot rage boiling in his belly. He grabbed the cup of coffee and slammed it into the sink, spraying coffee and pieces of porcelain mug all over the kitchen.

James stopped dead in his tracks, panting. He lifted a shaking hand and stared at the blood that oozed from his palm. One of the pieces of the mug had cut his hand, and only the piercing pain had halted his fit of anger. He pinched the bridge of his nose with his other hand and let out a quivering sigh.

This wasn't the man he really was. This wasn't the man that Suzie needed him to be, much less the man she would agree to marry. More than that, this wasn't the man that Johnny knew or would have been proud to call a friend.

He grunted as he grabbed a broom and began sweeping up the pieces of the whiskey bottle. This was his third bout of rage today, and it wasn't even 10 am. They had been coming along more frequently as the days went by, ever since that awful day in the desert. James was on a crash course to total self-destruction, he knew that. He also knew there was help available to him if he would only reach out for it.

He stopped sweeping for a minute and gazed out the kitchen window. The kind of help that he needed would require an inpatient stay, that much was correct. Before he made that leap, he needed to see Suzie. He needed to hold her one more time and tell her what was really going on.

* * *

James parked his truck in front of Suzie's house. She came running down the walkway, beaming, and threw herself into his arms before he could even get out of the driver's seat.

He laughed as she peppered his cheeks with little kisses. "Easy now, sweetie! We just did this whole thing yesterday, too!"

Suzie tossed her straight, red hair behind her shoulder as she grinned at him. "Yeah, but I've got to make up for ten months of missing you."

He smiled and planted a tender kiss on her lips. "I know the feeling," he whispered as he wrapped his arms around her waist. "On that note, can I talk to you about something?"

"Of course, baby." Suzie took his hand and led him to the front porch to sit.

James took a deep breath and locked his fingers with hers. "I've been having...issues since I got home."

She furrowed her brow and wrapped both of her hands around his. "What kind of issues?"

"Um," James rubbed the back of his neck, uncomfortably. "I've been having these tantrums, I guess. I haven't been sleeping. I keep having nightmares, and it's only getting worse." He suddenly felt a lump rise in his throat. He coughed, trying to clear it, and blinked back the tears that were pooling in his eyes.

"I, uh, ahem!" He swiped at his face. "I don't feel good about who I am these days, Suzie. And I want to be a good man for Johnny; he died fighting the same war I was and…" He let a few tears fall as he looked her in the eye. "I want to be a good man for you. You've been my guiding light since we were kids, and you deserve so much more than I can give you. I want to be a better man for you."

Suzie's tears fell freely as she wrapped her arms around James' neck. "Oh, honey. You're such a good man, the best man in the world. You've just been through hell and back. I love you, James. I will always love you, no matter what." She pressed her forehead to his.

James shook his head and smiled through his tears. "I love you, too, Suzie Oswald. I love you so very much." He pulled back so he could look her directly in the eyes.

"And that's why I've decided to get some help, serious help. There's an inpatient program for veterans. It's six months of treatment and rehabilitation. I've thought long and hard about it, and – I'm going there tomorrow."

Suzie sucked in her breath. She cupped James' face in her hands with a sad smile. "This is another battle that I know you can get through, and I'll be with you every step of the way. I am so proud of you, soldier."

James exhaled, letting out all the tension he had felt about having this conversation with her. "You'll still be my pen pal while I'm in there, right? I'll still get letters from you?"

She laughed and kissed his forehead. "Of course. I'll write to you every day, James Young."

* * *

James laid on his bunk, staring at the ceiling. Five months had passed since he entered the inpatient program. His official diagnosis was severe PTSD, the same as many other vets in the program with him. He had been working with doctors, psychiatrists, and mentors who were also veterans. This process was the hardest thing he had ever done in his life, even with three tours in the Middle East.

As promised, Suzie wrote him letters regularly. They had stopped coming as frequently in the last couple of weeks, but James didn't blame her. Suzie was balancing her full-time job, her passion project, and her overbearing parents.

James smirked as he thought of the disgust on Bryan Oswald's face, Suzie's father, when James would ask for Suzie's hand in marriage. Mr. Oswald believed that James was nothing more than a poor, broken soldier, Suzie's childhood flame that was long overdue to be extinguished. He had even gone so far as to set Suzie up on a date with Robert King, the son of Mr. Oswald's rich golfing buddy. Bryan was crystal clear about what he wanted for his daughter's life – and even clearer about what he didn't want.

James rolled over and pulled a shoebox full of Suzie's letters out from underneath his bed. He propped himself up against the wall as he reread the most recent one.

My dear James,

I cannot wait until I see you again. These days are getting harder with every passing one. Daddy insists that I'm wasting my youth and need to settle down with a "provider." He says I shouldn't be wasting my time with silly paintings. Can you imagine? He's trying to get me to go out with that abhorrent Robbie King again – the dull-brained jock. The only reason that man is going to be successful is because he's going to inherit his daddy's business empire with his daddy's trusted advisors, and all he has to do is smile and look pretty – ugh! The man won't do an honest day's work for once in his life! And can I just say, asking a woman, "Did it hurt when you fell from heaven," is NOT going to get you far at all. Oh yeah! He asked me that question at the charity gala last weekend! And sadly, that wasn't the first time.

But enough about him, that's not why I'm writing. I miss you something awful, James Young. I really do. Mama says you're a good man but that I should move on, but I don't believe her for a second. I think you're going to do great things in this life, and I want to be right by your side when you do them. So just hurry up and get back here, okay? And maybe send some extra letters once in a while?

I'm trying to hang in there, honey. It's just getting hard out here without you. Come home soon.

All my love,
Your Suzie

James sighed as he dropped the letter back into the box. That pretty much summed up most of her recent letters – her father pushing her into the arms of Robert King, her mother pushing her away from art and James, and Suzie caught in the middle of it all. The poor girl was being squeezed so hard she was bound to pop any day now.

James went to the desk on the other side of his room and pulled out a pen and paper to write her back.

Dear Suzie,

Have you tried socking this Robbie guy right in the nose? Sure, it would get in the way of him smiling and looking pretty, but it may be worth it.

I'm sorry that things have been so hard lately. I know the feeling. To be honest, I've wanted to give up so many times during this program because it's been so taxing. But you know what? Every time I picture your gorgeous face and your beautiful smile, it somehow makes everything better. Every day is still hard, but I have a damn good reason to keep pushing forward – that reason is you, Suzie Oswald.

Only a few more weeks until I'm clear, baby girl. Then we can get started on our life together. Just hang in there a little bit longer.

Love,
James

Three weeks later, James came out smiling after meeting with the program manager. James burst into his room and scrambled to pull out a pen and paper. He was breathing heavily and shaking, but in the best of ways. The program manager had just confirmed that he was cleared for release, a whole week earlier than expected! He couldn't wait to tell Suzie the news – he couldn't wait to see her again. It had been weeks since he last heard from her, which he found a little odd, but was just too excited to see her to start worrying.

He didn't bother sitting. He stood at the desk and scribbled furiously.

Dear Suzie,

I've got fantastic news, sweetheart – I'm busting out of here! I haven't had an anger attack in weeks, and therapy has been going so well, the program manager gave me the green light! Since I've been such a good little patient, they're letting me out a whole week early!

I'll be leaving three days from now, on June 13th. At 6 pm, I'll be in downtown Myrtle Beach at our favorite restaurant. You remember – the one we used to go to as kids? Jack's Crab Hole? Meet me there on the patio. I'll be waiting. Then, we can finally start our new life together.

We did it, baby girl. We're on the other side. Nothing but blue skies and sunshine from here on out.

I love you so much, Suzie Oswald. See you soon.
James

This was it, the beginning of the rest of his life. He was going to live every day for Suzie. He was going to make Johnny proud and settle down with the woman of his dreams. The first thing he was going to do was get himself a ring and make Suzie his forever partner, and their favorite restaurant in Myrtle Beach was the perfect place to do it.

James rushed to the mailroom to send his letter to Suzie, a giant smile on his face. He laughed out loud with glee as he ran – this was the best day of his life.

***

Three days later, James sat on the patio of Jack's Crab Hole. He checked his watch: 6:15 pm. No sign of Suzie, but he was optimistic. They had waited for this day for so long. She was bound to show. He pulled a small box out of his pocket and opened it under the table, just to be safe. A small, gold ring glinted in the evening light. It was tiny, and it didn't cost much, but it was all he could afford at the moment. He would rather propose now with a small ring than wait any longer, and he resolved to get Suzie a bigger ring as soon as possible.

He snapped the box shut with a sigh and looked around the patio for the hundredth time – still no Suzie. He rechecked his watch: 6:19 pm. A tiny surge of fear pricked at his heart. Suzie hadn't answered any of the letters he sent recently. Maybe she had moved on. Maybe Robbie King won after all.

He shook his head to clear his head. *No,* James thought to himself. *She'll be here soon. I just know it.*

But hours passed, and Suzie didn't show up. James was worried now, and he decided to take matters into his own hands. He paid his tab for the few sodas and appetizers he had consumed while he waited then piled into his truck. He needed to go to her house and see what was up. He needed to know why she didn't come.

Suzie's house was dark when James arrived, except for one lamp glowing in the living room window. James parked in the driveway behind Suzie's shiny silver Cadillac. He cautiously made his way up the front steps and raised his hand to knock. He hesitated. What if she had decided she didn't love him anymore? What if he had taken too long?

Ultimately, James decided that knowing for sure was better than always wondering, so he firmly knocked on the heavy wooden door.

As the door swung open, a flood of words came pouring out of James' mouth. "Hi, Suzie, I'm so sorry just to be barging in on you, but I sent you that letter and wanted to – oh."

He stopped short.

Standing at the door was Charlene Oswald, Suzie's mother. Her face was drawn and pale. She clutched a wad of tissues in her hand, and her eyes were red. She sniffled, and a fresh wave of tears streamed down her face when she saw it was James.

"Um, hello, Mrs. Oswald." James nodded his head respectfully, still puzzled by her presence. "I, uh...is Suzie home?"

Mrs. Oswald choked back a sob and pressed the tissues to her nose. James' stomach began to churn. Something was clearly wrong – very wrong.

"Mrs. Oswald—"

"I'm so sorry, James. Come in, please." Charlene opened the door wider and ushered him inside.

Inside Suzie's house, boxes were strewn across the floor, some half-filled, and some completely taped up. Half of the usual furniture was missing, and several of Suzie's paintings were leaning against the wall.

Mrs. Oswald guided him to a single armchair sitting in the corner. "Please, sit," she whispered.

James slowly sat, tentatively looking around the bare room. He wiped his sweating palms on his pant legs and felt the ring box in his pocket. "Mrs. Oswald, is everything alright? Where's Suzie?"

Charlene said nothing. She made her way to one of the open boxes in the room and pulled out a stack of papers. She sifted through them, sniffling and dabbing at her eyes as she went. She pulled out a letter from the middle of the pile. With a shaking breath, she brought it to James and placed the letter in his hands. It was addressed to James at his rehabilitation center.

He looked up at Mrs. Oswald, but she dropped her eyes to the floor, fiddling with her tissues.

James swallowed hard and opened the letter with a quaking hand. He unfolded the paper and began to read:

My dearest James,

It breaks my heart into millions of pieces to write this letter, but it's the only way I will ever find closure. I am so sorry, my love. I'm sorry that I wasn't there for you more. I'm sorry that I couldn't support you well in your final battle. I'm sorry that I wasn't enough for you.

You were such an amazing man, James Young. Your smile lit my heart up like fireworks on the Fourth of July. Your heart was so big it could hold the world. You say that I was your guiding light, but really you were mine. If it weren't for you, I would have accepted my fate and wholly given up on my art. But you told me that the world needed my beauty, and that fanned my creative flame. I'm sorry that I couldn't do the same for you.

I love you, James. You were the one thing keeping me going in this life. Now that you can't do that, I don't know how much longer I can hold on.

When we meet in the next life, I promise that I will hold you tightly and never let go. You're my hero, James. Always and forever.

All my love,

Your Suzie

James lowered his arm, dropping the letter to the floor. He felt the panic in his stomach morphing into a boiling rage for the first time in months. He squeezed his hands into fists and pressed them into his knees as hard as he could, trying to suppress his swirling emotions.

"Mrs. Oswald," he said gravely, "she said that I *was* an amazing man. She apologized that she wasn't there for me in my 'final battle.' What the hell does this letter mean?"

Mrs. Oswald covered her mouth to stifle a sob that rose in her throat. "Oh, James." She squeaked out. "It was Bryan. It was all his idea, and I went with it. How I wish that I hadn't, but I did."

"What do you mean, Mrs. Oswald? What did you go with?" James pounded a fist on his leg.

She wailed and turned her back to him. "I'm sorry! Oh Lord, how sorry I am!" She hugged her arms to her stomach. "Bryan figured out that you were writing to each other while you were in rehab. He was furious, and I couldn't talk him down off that ledge. So, he began intercepting your letters before Suzie could read them."

James froze. The rage in his stomach surged, but he fought it back. "What do you mean?"

Mrs. Oswald turned, looking sadly into his eyes. "He took some of the letters that you've been writing each other. And, well..." She reached inside the box again and pulled out a stack of letters held together by a rubber band.

James jumped up from the chair and swiped the stack of letters out of her hands. He tore the rubber band off and madly sorted through the envelopes, checking the dates stamped on the corners — all the letters he had sent to Suzie in the last month.

"DAMMIT!" He hurled the letters against the wall, sending them fluttering into the air. Mrs. Oswald sobbed and turned her back to him again, holding her head in her hands.

James rushed over to her. "What does she think happened to me? Huh? What did you tell her?"

Mrs. Oswald squeaked her words out between sobs. "He – he… Bryan told Suzie that you overdosed. He told her that you passed away in rehab."

All of the color drained from James' face. His ears burned, and adrenaline began coursing through his veins. "She…she thinks I'm dead?"

Mrs. Oswald only sobbed.

James shook his head, vehemently, "No. No! No, she can't think that I failed! She has to know the truth! Where is she?" James grabbed her arms and shook her, causing Mrs. Oswald to wail louder. James released her from his grip and began running through the house, shouting. "Suzie! Suzie, are you here?! Come on, Suzie, it's me!"

"She's not… HERE!" Mrs. Oswald screamed. She melted onto the floor, her body wracked with sobs as she knelt on her hands and knees.

James flew back into the room and stood over here, shaking with anger and fear. "Mrs. Oswald. Please! Tell me where she is!"

Mrs. Oswald rocked back onto her knees and clutched her stomach. "She isn't here anymore."

"No shit," James muttered. He turned and punched a hole in the wall. "No SHIT, so where is she, then?! Huh?! Tell me!" he thundered.

Mrs. Oswald clutched her head and squeezed her eyes shut tight. She whispered something that James could barely make out. He flung himself to the floor in front of her.

"What? Say it again. Tell me where Suzie is."

Charlene opened her eyes and stared fearfully into James' eyes. "She's dead," she whispered again.

James fell back, stunned. "Wha-what? No." He shook his head again and began tugging at his hair, quickly losing control of his emotions. "No, she's not dead! How could she be dead?"

Mrs. Oswald took a breath and said softly, "She's dead because she killed herself. The lie that her father told was too much for her to bear. She couldn't stand the thought of living a life without you in it, so she took her own. My husband's stupid pride and meddling caused our daughter's death. She's gone, James. She's dead."

James could barely see anything as redness filled his vision. He felt like his heart had leaped into his head and was pounding furiously in his brain. The swirling fury in his stomach was boiling up, even more, threatening to spill over. He felt chills all over his body, shaking as if a high fever had just set in.

James ran out of the house and quickly got in his truck. Blinded with anger and despair, he had no destination in mind. But somehow, he ended up near the beach. He needed to be near the water. He got out of his truck and started walking towards the water. The moon seemed so big.

He thought of Suzie and the future he had in mind for them and sobbed. Clutching the small box in his hand, he slowly walked towards the water, towards the moon. Away from the people who destroyed them, away from the world that hurt them so. But he knew that this was not the ending that Suzie would have wanted for him. He walked back to shore and laid himself on the sand, looking up at the sky. Suzie was somewhere there, looking out for him, and maybe, just maybe, everything would be all right.

SOMEBODY'S WATCHING ME

We were moving to the city of skyscrapers, rude mannerism, and delicious pizza when I realized my life was going to become something peculiar. I thought a new school, new friends, and more of my mother's ridiculous obsession with nagging so much was going to be the most of my problems. I truly had no idea what was waiting for me in our new Brooklyn home until it was too late.

I uncurled the covers from my chin as a lightning bolt split the dark sky in half. The rain pattered against my bedroom window as the moonlight shined against my sheets. If there's anything I hated most about a storm, it's the darkness it brings with it, the ominous thoughts and beliefs that only plague people who are in the midst of pissing their pants. However, it wasn't the rain or the thunder or the shadow of my windowpane on my wooden floor that frightened me that night. It was the presence that was hidden in the shadows of my room, walking back and forth in front of my bedroom door. Whoever, or whatever it was, it didn't intend on leaving. If it was human, it didn't speak. It seemed only to pace back and forth. With each step, the floorboards whined and creaked. I convinced myself that there was a small possibility that one of my parents suddenly took up sleepwalking and I had to take that chance.

"Hello?"

It stopped.

But it didn't stop outside. The presence was a lot closer. It stopped right at the foot of my bed. I could feel it. I slowly crawled up to the headboard of my bed. My heart throttled against my chest. Adrenaline filled and flowed through my veins.

It breathed.

Its breath was coarse, heavy, almost a grunt or a growl. Deep and grumbling. I peered at the floor and noticed that within the shadow of my window's design stood a dark figure with what appeared to be long hair. It couldn't be real. It couldn't possibly be real. Each glance I took made me shiver. My eyes shifted from inside the blanket then back on the shadow on the floor. It didn't make any sense.

A ghost.

It had to be. It had to be a ghost, but why? Why might a ghost visit me? What could I possibly have done to --. My bedroom room opened, and the golden light in the hallway flooded onto my bedroom floor.

"Ma!" I exclaimed, trying to gather my thoughts. "There's a—"

"What are you doing in here?" she asked, rubbing her eyes with a sigh in her voice. "Stop walking around, Darren. I'm tired already from the move and need to be up early."

"But Ma, it wasn't m—"

"Get some sleep, Darren." She shakes her head and shuts the door.

My mom never believed anything that ever sprouted from my mouth. Most of the time, I felt like the boy who cried wolf. Could never get a word out, yet the minute she started to nag, I had to be her audience, grounded to a chair to listen. Thankfully, when the evening came, darkness filled my bedroom once more, there were no shadows or sounds. But...

I couldn't sleep.

For the longest time, it felt like I stared at the wall for hours, waiting for the sun to come up, but the sun abandoned me. The moon was out longer than it should be. The small glimmer of light did help a little bit as it coasted through my window and into my room. It wasn't until I started staring at the stars that I began to feel my eyelids closing by themselves. I could finally get some sleep.

I was wrong.

The moment I felt myself starting to drift from this world and into a deep slumber, my bedroom door opened. Footsteps started echoing throughout the room and, with it, a large shadow. The moment that I almost caught a glimpse of the shadow's source, the light in the hallway turned off. I threw the covers off, and I don't know if it was courage or stupidity that led me to follow the shadow. I peeked through my parent's half-open bedroom door and found them fast asleep.

The footsteps came from downstairs. There was certainly an intruder. When I got to the bottom of the steps, I flicked on each light and made our home as bright as it could be at 3:33am, looking at the clock. I didn't plan to go anywhere past the bottom step. I only listened in silence, waiting for the ghost to start venturing around again, but nothing. I sat there for almost an hour, slouching against the handrail, dozing on and off. The next thing I knew, my mother was waking me up the next morning.

A few days had passed and nothing. No signs of any ghost or intruder, I started to feel better about myself, more energized. But I'd be damned if I let my guard down. Though I still felt a singe of paranoia most of the time, finding it difficult to do my homework. Every few minutes or so, I'd find myself shifting in my chair and looking at the kitchen table, feeling eyes beaming into my back only to find nothing or no one there. A few times, I might have watched my own shadow, almost feeling as if it no longer belonged to me, possessed by the ghost. I needed to keep myself sane. Somehow. So, I thought maybe I could help Dad with a few of our unboxed things. It helped. Kept me busy for a time, but everything changed when the phone rang.

"Hello?" I heard Ma say as I sat at the table, "Hey, Missy."

Aunt Melinda? She rarely calls. The last we heard from her was

Christmas. She only comes around or talks to us when it's convenient for her, a holiday, or if something went horribly wrong.

I was able to scratch off one of the three possibilities. It wasn't a holiday. So, either she wanted something, or Ma was going to hearing some bad news. When Aunt Melinda wanted something, Ma would always sigh then roll her eyes…in that exact order. When it was bad news, Ma would bring her hand to her stomach and her shoulders would rise almost to her ears and she'd ask Aunt Melinda to, "Say that again."

I stopped working for a moment, waiting for my mother to say something, but it seemed as though she only listened. Then, after a while, she cupped her hand to her stomach and raised her shoulders.

"Say that again," she said.

Something horrible happened.

"Alright, we'll be there soon." She hung up the phone and paced for a while before stepping into the kitchen. She didn't seem as upset as usual; rather, she seemed more curious than worried.

"Everything alright, Ma?" I asked her.

"Aunt Missy asked that I come by immediately. Wouldn't say what was wrong. I'm going to check on her, just to be sure she's alright. Will you be alright by yourself for a few hours?"

"Yeah," I said. "I'll be fine. Clifton isn't too far from here, but tell her I said hi."

Ma nodded, and the worry on her face only increased as she walked away. When my dad came home, Ma shared the news, and he was more than understanding to leave immediately after a long day of work. She loved Dad for that. It didn't matter how big or small an issue was, if my mother had any issues at all, he catered to it without question. The only problem is, whenever I had an issue, I was "blowing things out of proportion," and the issue I was facing was that they were leaving me alone.

As the evening went by, I spent much of it watching an old horror classics like *Evil Dead*. I just love the old 80s horror films. The amount of gore, the guts, the ridiculously bad acting is far too entertaining to pass up, but I had plenty to learn from those films…like there's nothing more horrific than being alone when you know there's a chance that you actually aren't.

Three hours had gone by, and Ma only updated me with a simple text message.

"We'll be back in the morning. We arrived at your Aunt's. Your Grandma isn't feeling too good. We'll stay the night to take care of her."

I was very close with my Grandma when I was child, but I haven't seen her in years. I suddenly felt a little sad. I was her favorite grandson. Well, I was the only one. I said a little prayer and replied to her message.

"Okay. I send her my love. I hope she feels better," I replied.

Right after I sent the message, I realized that one thing was clear. I would be home alone overnight for the first time...*ever*.

The text message was almost a cue for the paranormal and supernatural world to invade mine. It truly felt like eyes dug into my back, random wisps of air brushed against the nape of my neck, sending goosebumps up my arms.

I wasn't alone. I couldn't possibly have been alone.

When I turned off the television, I thought I might have seen a shadow cast by, but it was just me being paranoid. The reflection of our window curtains blowing in the soft breeze of the night startled me. I hurried and closed all the windows, making sure that, if it weren't a ghost, but a tangible, living person, they couldn't get in.

I was wrong again.

The far wall made an unusual sound, one that made every strand of hair stand on my skin.

Nails. Sharp nails, tapping and clinking against it from the other side, but when I peered through the window curtains, no one was there. Something must've been *in* the wall. I stood before it, glaring at the wallpaper, expecting for it to happen again, but there was nothing.

"I'm losing my mind," I said. "I'm losing it."

I shook my head and sighed. A few moments later, another breath of air brushed against me. I looked around in dismay, but I didn't see the source. Suddenly, I realized that a window was open again. I picked myself up quickly and rushed to the kitchen. Without thinking, I grabbed a knife, convincing myself that I could somehow cut the ghost at the exact moment it attacked me. Simple physics. If it can touch me, it would have to materialize and enter the physical realm for a short time, and maybe I could hurt it too. That's what I thought at least. I did feel a little safer carrying it around. I suddenly had enough courage to walk through the house, peering around every corner in every room to be sure I was in fact alone.

Nothing.

"I know you're here," I said, out loud. "I don't know what you want, but whatever it is, please…If you need my help or something, can you just write it down instead of scaring me?"

What am I saying?! Well, maybe it's a civil ghost with good manners? That's a sketchy line of thought even for me. I berated myself for thinking of something like that. It was more suicidal than anything. I took a breath and tried to relax, but it didn't help much. Several minutes and seconds went by. But time didn't help me.

I just need some fresh air, I thought. That's all I need. Yeah. Some fresh air and I'll be fine. I decided that it might be better to put some distance between me and the house and some pizza. Why was I thinking of pizza at a time like this?

There's never a bad time to think of pizza!

I quickly grabbed my hoodie in case it was going to start raining again and headed down the street to an old pizza joint I saw while walking home. I felt better already, smelling the warm, crusted bread in the oven and hearing voices besides my own frightened thoughts. If I could stay the night here, I would, but once I got my box, it was time to head back. Already, I felt my gut clench and tighten with every step I took towards home. Maybe it wasn't so bad. Maybe the ghost would share a pizza with me. When I rounded the final corner, my phone buzzed. Ma was calling.

"Ma?" I answered, carrying my rectangular pizza box.

"Darren…" she said, and her voice cracked as she said my name.

"Everything alright?" I asked, slowing down my pace to listen.

"Your father thought it be best I let you know what has happened."

"Okay…What's going on?" I finally got back to the house and stopped just before the steps.

"Well," Ma said, "I wished to tell you sooner, but I didn't want you to deal with this at home on your own."

"Deal with what, Ma? What are you talking about? How's Grandma?"

She sighed through the phone, and it took her a while before she could respond. That's when I heard it. That's when I heard the cry in her voice.

"Grandma passed away," she said, her voice hoarse.

My world shattered beneath my feet as I felt eyes on me again from the house. I traced where I felt the eyes were coming from and raised my head. The box of pizza slipped from my shaking hands. The tomato and cheese splattered across the pavement, but it wasn't just the revelation of what happened to my grandma that forced me to drop the pizza. It was the fact that when I looked up at my bedroom window as Ma continued to speak, my grandma was looking right at me.

EVEN THE NIGHTS ARE BETTER

After what felt like an eternity, Bill Hayward had finally touched down at the JFK airport. It felt good to stretch his legs. Being as tall as he was, airplanes weren't exactly the most comfortable form of travel, but he had dealt with the discomfort on account of his best friend. Arturo was once the star running back for their high school team. As the quarterback, Bill had depended on Arturo to be at his best, and during their senior year, they were on fire, bringing the team to the state championships. Winning that trophy had bonded them for life, which meant that Bill was now required to attend Arturo's wedding even if traveling all the way to New York from California was a bit of a hassle.

Like everyone else, he made for the carousel to claim his baggage. The conveyer belt was already in motion, but it remained empty. People who were too impatient to stay still inched towards the beginning of the track, crowing around it, hoping theirs would be the first bag to appear. Instead, most people were disappointed when a little pink bag popped up and a five-year-old with pigtails rushed up to grab it. From that point, the bags kept coming, but Bill's seemed to be hiding at the bottom of the barrel because, even when the crowd thinned out, he was left standing there.

"Hey."

Bill looked up and spotted a familiar face.

"Bill, isn't it? Arturo's friend, right?" She held his gaze for a moment before her attention returned to the carousel. "I made the mistake of bringing generic-looking bags. It's so hard to tell what's mine and what isn't."

"You're supposed to tie a colorful piece of ribbon to one of the handles," said Bill. "It helps."

"I'll have to keep that in mind."

"But to answer your previous question, yes, the name's Bill. I'm assuming you're Diana. I've heard a lot about you from Sheila. Last I heard, you were living in the UK with your longtime boyfriend. It must be nice living in London. I've always wanted to travel there myself, but I'm not a big fan of airplanes."

"Oh? But you took one here." Diana stepped forward and attempted to pull a bag off the carousel. As it turned out, her grip wasn't as firm as she thought it was and the bag slipped away. She was going to chase after it, but Bill swooped to the rescue. "Thanks," said Diana. Bill had made picking up her fifty-pound bag look so easy. "I'm impressed."

"So am I," responded Bill. "What do you have packed into this thing? A couple of bricks?"

"Something like that." Diana smiled. "Oh, there's another one of my bags. I'm on a roll."

Bill grabbed the second suitcase. "Do you intend to live here or something?" he joked. "Because Arturo and Sheila only booked the hotel rooms for the weekend."

"Actually, I'll be moving to San Francisco once the wedding is over."

Out of the corner of his eye, Bill spotted his bag, but he ignored it, finding that he wanted to spend a bit more time with Diana. For whatever reason, he wanted to know her story. "What happened to London, if you don't mind me asking?"

"No, it's fine," said Diana. "Things just didn't work out between me and my boyfriend. We were together for a long time, but I came to realize that we had been fizzling out for a while, but we stuck together just because it was convenient to do so, but there really wasn't anything left for us if we kept pushing the relationship, so we decided to go our separate ways. We sold the flat, and I managed to snag a job in San Francisco."

"No kidding." Bill felt kind of lame for presenting her with such a response. He rubbed the back of his neck and tried to think of something else to say, but there was no coming back from that. So, he grabbed his bag and checked the locks just to make it look like he was doing something.

"What about you?" she asked. "Last I heard, you were married."

Bill held up his hands. There was no ring on his finger. "We're both in the same wheelhouse. I was married to my wife for ten years, and while it wasn't a perfect marriage, I didn't think it would ever end in divorce, but then on our tenth anniversary, she dealt me the papers. Apparently, she couldn't stand the constant bickering, and my mannerisms were driving her inside." Bill shrugged, passing it off as no big deal even though he had spent many sleepless nights trying to figure out what he had done wrong, and of course, his wife had never bothered to give him a straight answer on the matter so, even now, he was left in the dark.

Diana could see the pain he was trying hard to hide. Knowing how hard it was to talk about a broken heart, she tilted her head toward the exit. "We could continue sharing our sob stories, or we could get a move on."

"I think I would rather get a move on," said Bill. He was glad Diana hadn't probed for any additional information on his failed marriage. Telling her as little as he had was painful enough, and he did not want to feel that particular wound open any wider. "So, what are you going to do in San Francisco?"

"I'll be working for a financial firm. I'm a loan broker by trade, but recently, I've changed my focus to buying and selling stocks. It's much more exciting because you never know how the market will react on any particular day."

"You any good at it?" Bill asked as they got in line, passports in hand. "You know, it seems harder to leave this place than to break out of Alcatraz. How many security checkpoints do we need? You'd think, if I was concealing something dangerous, those expensive body scans would be able to find it."

"Unless they don't really work and the airlines bought them with government bailout money because, why not?"

"What are you? Some kind of conspiracy theorist?"

"You should hear what I have to say about vending machines."

"Vending machines?" Bill questioned. "You really have a conspiracy theory on vending machines?"

"Definitely."

"I would love to hear it," said Bill. "This should be interesting at the very least."

She leaned in like she was about to share an earth-shattering secret, but she didn't even manage a single word before she cracked. Her laughter pealed through the air like a ray of sunshine. Bill laughed alongside side her, and even when he got a hold of himself, a smile remained on his face. He liked this Diana woman. Spending even a few minutes in her company had been enough to put him in a good mood.

"Phew, I didn't think we would make it out of there alive," said Diana just as soon as they stepped aside.

"Alive to sell stock another day."

"That's a good one. I think I might get it painted on a sign for my new office."

"Hey, if you're going to use my quote, I had better get some royalties."

"I'll tell you what," said Diana. "We're both going the same way, aren't we? I'll let you hitch a ride in my taxi."

"How about we split the fare?"

"Sounds fair to me." Diana flashed an amazing smile. Bill couldn't help but notice her radiance. It wasn't just the warmth behind her smile but her personality, too. She liked to laugh and so did Bill. He felt comfortable joking around with her, and she seemed to feel the same way. More than that, he admired the fact that she was still living her life with an upbeat attitude despite the hiccup in her eight-year relationship. No matter how strong a person is, a breakup is never easy – never.

He attempted to hail down a cab, but the taxi drivers seemed to think him invisible.

"Here, let me try." Diana stepped up to the curb. It did not take more than a second for a yellow cab to pull up beside her. She winked over her shoulder before getting in the back of the car. Bill shook his head and helped the driver load the luggage.

"So, is that some kind of superpower you've got? The ability to hail taxis at the snap of a finger."

"If I disclose too much, I'll be putting you in harm's way, so it would be best if you just stopped asking questions." Again, she attempted to hold a poker face, but it didn't take long for her expression of seriousness to break under the charm of a smile. "You know, I'm glad I bumped into you. I thought this trip would be something of a bummer, but if you keep making me laugh like this, I think I'll be able to survive."

"I have a few corny jokes if you'd like to hear them."

"Sure, let them rip. I'm always one for horrible punch lines. They are almost as good as cheap beer."

Bill felt the joke slip away.

She likes beer? he thought. *Really?* It seemed too good to be true, but he couldn't spot even a single speck of deception anywhere on her person. Maybe he was wrong, but Diana did not seem like the kind of person to tell a lie just to impress someone else.

"Maybe we could grab a couple of beers sometime." The words came rushing out of his mouth before he could even consider how such an offer might look from her perspective. "I mean, as friends. I know Arturo and you know Sheila, but we don't really know each other, and I think that's a shame, especially since we'll be living in the same city."

"Oh?"

"I'm the security guard for a financial firm. Who knows, maybe we're working in the same building and don't even know it."

"Provenance?"

Bill blinked. Had he heard her correctly? "Did you just say Provenance?"

"Yeah, the one on Suffolk St."

"What are the odds?"

"Wait, is that where you work?" asked Diana. "No." She grabbed his arm. "You're just pulling my leg."

"I'm not. Really." Bill pulled out his wallet and showed her this ID badge he wore to work every day. "See."

Diana took it from his hand. "Wow, that's crazy, isn't it? Maybe we should stop and play the lottery or something."

Bill chuckled. "Well, that depends on whether you'll consider yourself lucky to be working at Provenance and seeing my mug every day when you walk into the building. Although, if you get on my good side, I usually have some sort of unhealthy snack that I share with my friends."

"What kind of snacks are we talking about?"

"Donuts, muffins – you know, all the stuff your doctor doesn't want you to eat and, when they ask you about it, you always lie and say you've been eating your daily serving of vegetables."

"You make a valid point," said Diana. "It might be really hard to get along with someone who brings donuts to work."

They arrived at the hotel in what felt like no time at all, for they were both enjoying each other's company too much to notice. Bill got out of the car first and held open the door for Diana, even going so far as to offer his hand.

She took it, surprised to find a tingling underneath her skin at his touch. It crept up her arm and left her heart racing. Blush rose to her cheeks, painting them a soft shade of pink. Thankfully, Bill did not notice for he was already unloading her bags.

"Thanks." Diana led the way into the lobby. They checked into their rooms and stepped into the elevator.

Bill checked his room number before pressing the right button on the elevator's number pad. "Would you look at that," said Bill, "lucky number seven."

"Do you believe in that sort of stuff?"

"I think it's good to believe in something or you start to become lost," he answered. "It gives me something to hold on to – a ground if you will."

"I never thought about it like that."

"Well, most people only believe in luck when they're in Vegas."

"And we're a long way away from Vegas," said Diana.

"Exactly."

Diana's room was right across the hall from Bill's. "I'll see you at the wedding?"

"Unless I come down with some terrible illness between now and then, you can count on it," said Bill. "Have a good night."

"Goodnight." Diana slipped into her room. As soon the door closed behind her, she felt the weight of loneliness once more.

* * *

Bill turned his head and looked toward the window. He had forgotten to draw the blackout curtains, and as a result, the bright moonlight had penetrated his room, painting everything with a silver glaze. He watched the clouds get pushed around the nighttime sky by the invisible winds. There were times when watching the clouds roll over the moon could lull him to sleep, but tonight was not one of those nights.

He turned his head in the opposite direction so he could see the clock. 3:44 A.M. was illuminated by bright red numbering. In a couple of hours, he would need to get up and get ready for the wedding. He could only hope that he still remembered how to tie a tie. It had been quite a while since he had attended any sort of formal event. He just wasn't a suit and tie sort of guy. Perhaps it was one of the reasons his wife had chosen to leave. Perhaps she was sick and tired of never being taken out on a date night, but was he really to blame for enjoying a night in by the fire? He had even attempted to make those nights romantic with chocolates and champagne, but no matter what he did, it was never enough.

Whenever these thoughts reared their ugly head, Bill knew it meant another sleepless night. So, he got up and threw on some clothes, thinking that a bit of fresh air would help clear his mind. The halls were quiet with most people tucked away in their rooms. Bill tried not to think of all the happy couples who were soothed to sleep knowing that, come morning, their love would still ring true. Bill no longer had that luxury. Every morning, Bill was greeted by an empty bed -- a cruel reminder that he was no longer wanted by the women he had dedicated ten years of his life to. How could she just throw that away? The thing that stung the most about the whole affair was that she didn't even try to salvage the marriage. She was more than content to walk away and leave it all behind.

Bill felt his stomach tighten into a knot. He felt sick, and that nausea was made worse by the elevator. It jerked to a stop on the ground level and slowly opened its doors.

The young woman behind the check-in counter nodded her head in greeting. "Can I help you with anything, sir?"

Can you tell me what I did wrong? Can you tell me how I messed up in my marriage and how I drove away my wife? thought Bill, but of course, he did not voice these questions aloud. "Just taking a walk down to the beach."

"Enjoy," said the receptionist with a wave of her hand.

Outside, the air had a bit of a bite to it, sinking its teeth into his skin. He thought about returning to his room for a sweatshirt, but he couldn't be bothered. So, he slipped his hands into his pockets and wandered down the path. There was a bit of a hunch to his back as a result of his heavy shoulders. He felt like he was carrying the weight of the world on his shoulders — a punishment he had to bear for being a major screw up. If only he had paid attention to her more — listened to her more — spent the time to make her smile and laugh even in the later years of their marriage — maybe things would have been better.

But as much as Bill wanted to turn back the clock and fix his mistakes, that just wasn't possible. His ex-wife had made her decision to never see him again, and he just had to accept that.

The boardwalk was deserted when Bill got there. There were a few teenagers lingering about. Those that had ventured down to the water were even fewer. A few heads could be seen bobbing in the water, and there was a lone surfboarder catching the nighttime tide. Bill watched the surfboarder until he wiped out, disappearing underneath the waves.

Bill took off his shoes with the intention of dipping his toes in the water. He was just about to reach the water's edge when he noticed someone sitting nearby with their knees pulled up against their chest. It looked like a woman or a very small man, but he didn't know too many guys who would sit in such a manner. "Hey, are you okay?" Bill did not know what possessed him to ask the question, but it was out of his mouth. Already, he was turning toward the figure because there was something undeniably sad about the stranger, and Bill wanted nothing more than to try to help. Maybe a good laugh was all this person needed.

To his surprise, when the stranger pulled down her hood, it wasn't a stranger at all but someone who had been on his mind for most of the night.

"Diana?" he whispered her name as if saying it any louder would cause her to disappear. "What are you doing here? You should be back at the hotel where it's safe."

"I could say the same for you," said Diana. "You're out here as well, aren't you?"

Bill could not argue with that, so he approached her, hoping to spend more time by her side. Since they had gone their separate ways, Bill had been left with this hollow feeling in his chest like, somehow, his heart had been carved from his ribcage. "Mind if I take a seat?"

"Go right ahead, but I can't promise I'll be very cheerful company."

"I know we don't know each other that well, but if you want to get something off your chest, then I'm willing to listen." Bill sat down beside her and noticed how small she seemed, like she was on the verge of disappearing. "I'm here," he said, "so you don't have to be alone anymore."

Diana was quiet for a long while, but Bill did not push her to speak. Instead, he gave her the time to get comfortable – to sort through her thoughts before she tried to spell them out into words. "I know I mentioned my breakup as this casual thing, but really, it hit me harder than I ever thought it would. I always thought that I'd be able to stand on my two feet if anything happened, but right now, I just feel like disappearing into the water, never to be found again."

Bill placed his hand on her arm and gave it a gentle squeeze. She blinked like she was returning from some faraway place and looked up. Bill noticed the tears welling up in her eyes. He wanted nothing more than to wipe those tears away and see that gorgeous smile of hers, but he knew that running his thumb across her cheek might overstep some invisible barrier. So, he settled for wrapping his arm around her shoulders and giving her someone to lean on.

"I really don't know how it happened. In the beginning, we were so happy together. I thought, without a doubt, we had the sort of chemistry that would carry us through. Honestly, I thought he was the one. But then the years went by, and I saw a different side of him. He would work extra hours, and I swear, he used that as an excuse to get out of the house – to stay away from me. And I did my best to keep the relationship alive, but everything I did sparked a fight. Those last few years were more of a screaming contest than anything else, but I held on thinking things could change and be like they were." Her voice faded into the wind. She was crying. Bill could feel it in the shaking of her body – the tremor of her shoulders. He held her a little closer.

"Sounds to me like he forgot what a wonderful woman you are."

"You're just saying that," responded Diana. "You don't know me. I could have been a nightmare."

"I highly doubt that," whispered Bill. "It sounds to me like you did everything you could to salvage the relationship, but it just wasn't in the cards. You shouldn't beat yourself up over it. His loss will be someone else's gain – trust me." Gently, Bill placed a finger underneath her chin and lifted it so he could better see her eyes. "I'm not going to tell you to forget your ex-boyfriend because that's just not realistic. You spent eight years by his side. But I will tell you to move forward with your life. Take this move to San Francisco and this new job as a starting point. Explore new things. Pick up some new hobbies and just have some fun with your life because a girl like you shouldn't be crying the night away."

She found herself comforted by his gaze. Perhaps she didn't know this man all that well, but all the same, she was glad for his company. "What about you?" she asked. "What really happened with your divorce?"

"I think she was cheating," whispered Bill. It was the first time he had spoken his suspicion aloud. "But I never confronted her about it because I wanted to be the husband who trusted his wife. When she told me that she was going out with the girls, I chose to believe her because I didn't want to face some other reality."

Diana turned slightly so she could better see his face as he spoke. The pain was there, etched into every line. He too was making himself vulnerable, letting the truth become illuminated by the moonlight. "Was she? Cheating I mean."

"I don't know, and I don't intend to find out. I know that, if I do, I'll never be able to trust again. I'd rather just stay ignorant of what really happened. I signed the divorce papers and well, that's that."

"But don't you stay up at night wondering if there was something you could have done that would have saved the relationship?"

Bill actually laughed. "Why do you think I'm here?"

"Point," said Diana as she laughed alongside him. "How about we cut all this failed relationship talk and we move the conversation elsewhere?"

"I'm more than happy with that." Bill allowed his arm to come off her shoulders for he felt it was no longer appropriate for him to hold her in such a manner. He didn't want to for he quite enjoyed having someone near after a few months of nothing but loneliness. "Tell me why you came to sit by the ocean. Are you a fan?"

"Who isn't?"

"Those who don't know how to swim," answered Bill, "and those afraid of the water."

"Those are usually the same group of people," said Diana. "And I am not one of them. I love the water. I was part of my university's swim team."

"Were you any good?"

"I was decent. I was never a major record-breaker, but I pulled my weight, and I made sure never to let the team down." She got up and brushed the sand from her pants. "Walk with me?"

Bill obliged. "If we're talking sports, I used to be the quarterback for my high school."

"Right, I think I remember Sheila saying something about you and Arturo being on the same team. From what I've heard, you two were pretty good – brought home a championship trophy or something."

"Oh yes," said Bill. "That was my crowning achievement right there."

"Sometimes, don't you just wish you could be a teenager again? Life used to be so simple back then."

"That's because most teenagers think they have everything figured out and have no idea how naïve they truly are. When you're a teenager, love is so easy to understand because all you have to do is listen to the latest hit on the radio, but you don't think about the effect money has on a relationship or how your partner's little habits might drive you up a wall over time." Bill stopped abruptly, causing Diana to walk into him. They nearly toppled over, but Bill managed to steady himself and Diana too.

"Sorry," she whispered, becoming red in the face. "I guess I should look where I'm going."

"No, it's my fault," said Bill. "I shouldn't have stopped so suddenly, but would you look at that?" He picked up a conch shell. "You almost never find these things undamaged, let alone on a popular beach." Gently, he brushed Diana's hair behind her ear before holding up the shell so that she could hear its sound. "Is it true? Does it really sound like the ocean?"

She placed her hand on top of his and listened. "It does," she said with a smile. "Listen for yourself." With her hand still on his, she brought the shell to his ear, rising onto her tiptoes in order to do so.

"Looks like you've got yourself a souvenir."

"But you were the one to find it," protested Diana. "It's only right that you should have it."

"I want you to have it," he said. "Think of it as the symbol of your new life. Maybe the sound is a little fuzzy, but it's beautiful all the same.

You might not know what the future holds, but I have no doubt that you'll pave your own way and that it'll be a sight to behold."

He continued along the shore, leaving Diana to catch up, clutching the shell in one hand. "So, do you have any good football stories to tell me? Killer passes and last-minute touchdowns, perhaps."

"You don't have to pretend to like football just to humor me, you know."

"Who said anything about pretending? My father was a huge football fan. I practically grew up watching the sport, and I still watch it today."

"You do?"

"Every Sunday."

Bill stopped short once more, but this time, Diana was ready for it. She rocked back onto her heels and grinned, amused by the look on Bill's face.

"What? Is it really that strange to find a girl who is genuinely interested in football?"

"It isn't strange," said Bill. "It's amazing." From that point forward, the conversation flowed effortlessly, moving from topic to topic as if Bill and Diana had known each other for years. And it certainly felt that way when they called it a night and retired to their rooms. Neither Bill nor Diana had any trouble sleeping after that.

All too soon, Bill was roused from his dream, and what a wonderful dream it had been. He was back with Arturo, tearing up the football field, only he had made it to the college level, riding on a scholarship. In order to pass his classes, he had found himself a tutor. She was the smartest girl in the entire grade, and lucky for him, she happened to live across the hall. He had gathered up the courage to ask her for help, and soon, she was more than just a tutor. She went to his every game – his own personal cheerleader.

He woke up just before the team could score its winning touchdown to the sound of someone knocking on his hotel door. Still half-asleep, he got out of bed. He rubbed his eyes and looked through the peephole. To his surprise, his cheerleader was standing in the hall, holding the front of her dress and looking a bit flustered.

"Bill, please!" she called through the door. "I need your help!"

It was then that Bill came to realize that he had dreamt about Diana, the future bride's best friend. They had spent most of the night walking the shore and talking about this and that. It must have made an impression on his mind because what else could explain her appearance in his dreams?

Just before Diana could walk away, Bill opened up the door. "What's up?" He tried to keep a certain coolness to his voice, but he had a feeling that he was coming across more awkward than anything else. "Why are you all dolled up?"

"We have a wedding to go to, remember?"

His eyes widened. "Oh, shoot! You're right. I didn't think to set an alarm. Good thing you came knocking at my door."

Diana pushed herself into the room and turned around. "Would you mind zipping me up? I swear this dress was perfect when I bought it. I must be bloated from travel. Oh, I'm going to look terrible. Why did I ever think this type of dress was going to work with my body type?"

Bill did not know what she was talking about because, as far as he was concerned, she looked absolutely stunning. So, without a word, he silenced her fears by placing his hands on her shoulders. Once she was still, he slowly zipped up the back. "I think you look beautiful," he whispered.

She felt a bloodred warmth spreading across her cheeks and up to the very tips of her ears. "Do you really mean that?"

"I do. I think the dress looks lovely, and I like what you've done with your hair."

"I wasn't sure whether I would butcher curling my own hair, but I didn't want to spend an arm and a leg getting it professionally done, you know?"

"I don't blame you." Bill found it hard to look away from the woman that now stood in the middle of his room. He had noticed her beauty from the start, but paired with everything he had learned about her during the course of the night, it seemed to elevate that beauty and take it to a whole different level. "Do you know how to tie a tie?" he asked.

"Hmm?"

"Do you know how to tie a tie?" he repeated. "Because I have always been quite terrible at doing it myself."

"I can't say that I do, but I would be more than happy to look it up while you get dressed. Which, you should probably get a move on, or we're going to be late, and I don't want to face the wrath of a bridezilla."

"Right." Bill grabbed his clothes and disappeared into the bathroom.

As Diana waited, she found a few how-to videos online. Tying a tie seemed easy enough. Just to make sure, she grabbed Bill's tie and wrapped it around her neck, going through the motions, step by step. All seemed to be going well until she made that final tug and found that the ends were horribly uneven. She undid the knot and tried again but ended up with similar results.

"Any luck?" asked Bill.

Diana's jaw fell open the second she saw him. The security guard had cleaned up rather nicely. The suit he wore was a dark grey, which contrasted nicely with the white shirt underneath. The polka dot tie had seemed questionable when Diana first picked it up, but now, she saw how it might add to the look.

"Um..." She tried to get her brain back to working order, but it was difficult to put her thoughts to words when her heart was beating a mile a minute, sending an overload of blood to her brain. "You look nice," she said at last. "But we might have a little problem with the tie. I can't seem to figure out how to line up the ends."

"Let's give it a try and see what happens."

"Pop your collar for me." Diana stepped forward until they stood no more than a few inches apart. She could feel the heat coiling around her body, and it was only getting hotter. She reminded herself to breathe as she rose onto her tippy toes and placed the tie around his neck. "Alright, do me a favor and hold the phone for me."

Bill did as he was told.

Diana saw that her fingers were shaking. Again, she reminded herself to breathe, but it was easier said than done when her skin felt like it was on the verge of melting right off her face. Somehow, she managed to follow the video, and by some miracle, it came out okay. "It's not perfect," she said.

"But it's a lot better than what I would have done," interjected Bill. "Besides, the end of it will be hiding underneath my suit jacket most of the night."

"Let me redo it. I am sure I can make it better."

"I rather not chance it. Besides, we don't have a lot of time to spare." Before Diana could say anything else, he took her by the hand and dragged her out of the room. Without meaning to, he weaved his fingers against hers, and instead of letting go, he held onto her hand all the more because it felt inexplicably right to do so.

They jumped into the elevator, and still, their hands remained clasped together. It was only once they reached the lobby and saw everyone else that they released their hold because they didn't want anyone to get the wrong idea.

"Come on," said Bill. "Let's snag us some seats before we're stuck in the back."

Diana nodded and followed him into the hotel's chapel. It was a beautiful space decorated with flowers and silk bows. Large, stained-glass windows lined the perimeter, illuminated by the late-morning sun. "It's gorgeous in here…" Diana whispered aloud, for it felt like she had stepped into a dream. Every time she had imagined her own wedding, it was in a room just like this. Perhaps she would have changed the color scheme and some of the flowers, but the similarity was uncanny. She half-expected to look down and find herself wearing a wedding dress, but she was met with no such luck.

"It is," agreed Bill. "Sure beats the tiny chapel where I got married. If I had to do it all over again with someone else, then I'd definitely want to book a place like this. Can you imagine the pictures?"

"Yeah." Diana sat down, her legs feeling like they had turned to jelly.

Her heart felt like it was made of lead. She could barely stand it. She wanted to be happy for her friend and the fact that she had found the one, but what about Diana? What would happen to her now? If she couldn't get married after an eight-year relationship, how would she ever find her prince charming? Or would she never walk down the aisle wearing white?

All these questions kept haunting her throughout the ceremony. It was a beautiful ceremony – she couldn't deny that – but that was all the more reason why it had her so upset. By the time the couple exchanged their vows, Diana had full-on tears running down her cheeks. She just couldn't stop herself from feeling miserable. It was this overwhelming sense of defeat like she would never get to a point of happiness again because it had been taken away from her the second she decided to move to the US and leave her ex-boyfriend behind. Perhaps she could still make amends. Perhaps she could still salvage her broken relationship and have that happily ever after that she had always wanted.

But she knew it wouldn't work that way. Her ex-boyfriend was far from being the prince charming she wanted, and forcing a marriage out of him would only end in disaster.

Bill pulled the buttonhole from his suit and offered it to her as a handkerchief, thinking that the wedding had made her emotional, since many of the other girls in attendance were also crying.

She wiped at her tears, but they kept coming, her eyes red and raw – heartbroken.

As soon as the couple left, hand in hand, Diana excused herself to the bathroom. Bill got this feeling that something was wrong, so he followed her, standing outside the woman's bathroom for a while. Plenty of other girls came and went, but there was no sign of Diana.

"Hey, would you mind checking on someone for me? She's wearing a navy blue dress and matching heels. Her hair is curled." Bill had flagged someone going into the bathroom. "I would really appreciate it."

The woman nodded her agreement and disappeared behind the swinging doors. A few minutes later, she reappeared. "She's in a right state," said the woman. "Crying her eyes out in there. Maybe you should talk to her. No one else is in there. Just lock the door behind you."

"Thank you." Bill did just that. With the door locked, he turned the corner and found Diana sitting on a bench by all the sinks, his buttonhole still in hand. It was wet from all her tears. "Hey, what's wrong?" asked Bill in a voice soft and gentle. "I know the wedding was a nice one and all, but I have a feeling that something else is at work here." He ran his thumb across her cheek, wiping away her tears. "Please, talk to me, Diana. It pains me to see you cry like this."

"It's just…" She balled the makeshift handkerchief in her hand. "I feel like I'm never going to get the dream wedding I always wanted. When I started dating my ex-boyfriend, I thought he was the one, but obviously, I was wrong about that. What if I never get it right? What if I wind up alone?"

"That isn't going to happen," said Bill almost at once. Throughout the day, he had been thinking about everything that had happened, and maybe it was a little unorthodox for him to jump into a relationship so soon after his divorce, but he truly believed he could have a second shot at love with Diana. He told her as much and held his breath, fearing her reaction. Would she think him too forward? Would she laugh in his face?

"You?" she asked. "You mean you want a relationship with me?"

"That's what I'm saying." Bill took both her hands. "And I know it might seem crazy because we barely know each other, but I think I've seen enough of your heart to know it is something I can cherish, so if you're willing to take a risk, so am I."

Diana looked into his eyes for only a moment before nodding her head. "I'm willing to try to make it worth," she said. "Because a happily ever after with you does sound pretty sweet."

"No arguing there," responded Bill with a grin. "So, does that mean I get to kiss you now? Because I'll tell you, I've been holding back since the moment I saw you —"

It looked like Bill was going to say something more, but Diana interrupted him by leaning forward. Their lips came together like fireworks.

Oh, thought Diana, *this is how it was always meant to be.*

At the reception, Bill and Diana found the happy couple and gave them their warm wishes. "It was a beautiful ceremony," said Diana.

"It had half the crowd in tears," added Bill as something of a joke. "I was tearing up a bit myself."

"I'm sure," answered Arturo. "I haven't seen you cry for anything except that one time you broke your ankle and you thought you would never walk again."

"Hey, the bone was practically sticking out of my skin. I had every right to cry."

Both girls flinched. "He's being dramatic," explained Arturo. "Sure, his ankle was bent a funny sort of way, but there weren't any bones to be seen."

"Um… perhaps we could change the topic of conversation," said Sheila, "like the fact that you two ran off together after the ceremony was over. Don't pretend like it didn't happen because I saw Bill chase after you. What was that about?"

"She had dropped her handkerchief. I was just being a gentleman and returning it to her."

Sheila and Arturo exchanged a knowing look before they excused themselves, wanted by another pair of guests.

"Shall we find our seats?" asked Bill as he held out her arm.

She took it, cheeks becoming rosy in color. "Hopefully they didn't sit me with all the kids. Sheila would probably think that's funny."

"Looks like you're with me," said Bill as he picked up both their name cards. "Lucky number seven."

"Do you think they had a hand in all this?" asked Diana.

"Hmm?"

"Well, they had our hotel rooms right across the hall and now they have us sitting together. Do you think they were trying to play at matchmakers?"

"If they were, I don't mind it. You might think me too optimistic for saying this, but I really do think we'll make a good match. I mean, I can't tell what the future will hold, but I have high hopes that it will remain as bright as it is now." Bill kissed the top of her head before pulling out her seat. "After you, my lady."

"Aren't you the gentleman," she commented, the rosiness of her cheeks becoming a shade darker.

"I try my best."

Soon, they were joined by members of Arturo's and Sheila's family – a couple of cousins and a lone uncle, who soon disappeared to the open bar. Friendly chatter floated across the table as everyone enjoyed their meal.

Arturo and Sheila cut their cake, making quite the mess of it. Beside Bill, Diana giggled. "I always thought that the cake-in-the-face bit was adorable – to see a couple laugh like that and be totally comfortable with one another…"

"Yeah," answered Bill, "I can see what you mean." He thought back to his own wedding. His wife had been so stiff throughout the whole thing and, at the time, he had just shrugged it off as wedding day nerves, but maybe it was more than that. Maybe her stiffness was the first sign that their marriage was never meant to be. With this thought, he vowed, if there ever came a day when he could take Diana for his wife, he would definitely throw some cake in her face. And he hoped that she would throw some cake in his, too.

"What are you smiling about?"

"Hmm?" Bill looked over at Diana. She was the only one left at the table. All the others had left during his daydream.

"You're smiling like an idiot over there, and I'm wondering what you're smiling about. Let me in on the secret," she whispered, leaning nice and close.

He thought about kissing her, but he didn't know how she felt about public displays of affection, so he kept himself in check, choosing to tease her instead. "Oh, nothing," he said with a sly grin.

"Oh, come on. You're obviously thinking of something to be smiling like that. Why won't you tell me?"

Bill just kept smiling.

"Fine." Diana crossed her arms and pretended to pout.

Bill answered her pout by pushing his uneaten slice of cake in Diana's direction. "It's all yours if you can find it in your heart to forgive me."

"Forgiven," she said. "This is some really good cake. You're missing out."

But Bill didn't care about missing out. It was enough to see Diana smiling. That, to him, was sweeter than any buttercream frosting.

As the night wore on, Bill and Diana kept each other company, talking about this and that because they found it impossible to tire of each other. But then, all of a sudden, Diana stopped midsentence and grabbed hold of Bill's arm.

"What?" asked Bill, alarmed, thinking that something was wrong.

"Come with me," she said. "I want to dance." She was already bobbing her head to the beat of the song. It was one of her favorites.

"Dance?" Bill was being dragged to the dancefloor, but halfway there, he dug his heels into the ground. "I'm not a very good dancer."

"Doesn't matter," said Diana with a mischievous glint to her eyes. "All I want is an excuse for you to hold me."

And there was no arguing with that.

While Bill's dance skills were questionable at best, the newfound couple danced the night away, holding each other tenderly.

BABY

Thighey had met in a wine bar seven years before. Jazz music rang through the speakers. Glasses were raised, and strangers laughed together.

"Wow," he said when she squeezed past. The tight red dress looked like a second skin over her narrow waist and curved hips.

She lifted her gaze from the swarm of bodies she was trying to push through behind two friends. Her eyes were hazel brown cut through with shards of gold.

"Excuse me, miss, for the last 30 seconds since you entered, I think I may have developed a crush on you. Let me buy you a drink," he stated and was not asking.

He smelled of pine. Evergreen eyes and hair the russet of a fading sun, he was stubbly with thin lips. There was a scar on his cheekbone. She didn't immediately fancy him - *Why is he wearing a plaid shirt?* - but he wasn't unattractive.

"Sofía!" her friend shouted.

"I'll catch up," she called in her Spanish accent.

"What will it be?" he asked.

"A mojito," she said, looking at the man carefully. She actually wanted an espresso or something else that would keep her going, but it would have been weird if the bar had it. But she knew she was tired and urgently needed caffeine. Being a secretary meant having a caffeine addiction. Mojito was fresh, though, and would make her mouth minty.

After they both got drinks, the two of them moved to a table on the floor above. Immediately, they started to click. They spoke about the most random things, environmental issues, the cost of a double shot cappuccino, and even had a debate on the length of her dress.

"It should be shorter," he quipped.

"You're cheeky." The mojito started to give her a red glow in her cheeks. "If you could be any animal in the world, what would you be?"

"A monkey," he said.

Cute, she thought grinning. *I haven't smiled this much since I was a kid.*

"What about you?" he asked.

"A labradoodle dog," she said.

He laughed. "But you're so elegant."

The look in his eyes changed from seductive to impressed. He loved her wild black hair that was gripped around her head, like a thunder cloud.

"You're cute," he said, standing. "I'm getting you another drink."

The trousers he wore were flecked in bits. Wood.

He saw her notice and explained, "I came straight from work. I'm a tree surgeon."

A man that climbs trees? Now that is sexy, she thought.

When he saw the smirk press her mouth, he knew he'd take her home that evening.

Marcus wasn't overly romantic, but within a week, he had already fallen deep within Sofía's charms. Sofía was standoffish after that evening, but after a while, she too fell in love with Marcus. Less than a month later, the two moved in together, and that evening, Marcus found himself in a jewelry store, buying a white-gold engagement ring. But he had to pick the right time to propose. He was sure she wanted to be with him. However, there was a certain timing for these things. After a few days, she was kneeling in his garden, absentmindedly pulling weeds from the flower bed while on the phone to her sister. He watched her from the window, trying to eavesdrop on their conversation. He overheard her saying, in answer to a question, "Of course, we'll get married one day. I think he's the one."

That same day, he brought the ring home, which he kept at his office for the past few days. But he didn't realize that she would be home early. He was stuck with the ring in his pocket trying to figure out where to put it. Frantic, he went upstairs right away and immediately went to the bathroom and locked the door behind him.

In the cupboard under the sink, he removed aftershave from its box and hid the ring box inside. It would do until Sofía left for work tomorrow morning. When he exited the bathroom, the smell of garlic filtered up from the kitchen and filled his nose.

Downstairs, Sofía was cooking cazuela with corn, chicken and potato. She was cooking more and more, practicing for when she became a mother, which was becoming closer and closer.

I need to tell him soon, she thought.

"How was your day, darling?" he said casually as he walked up behind her. His mouth was at her ear, his hands firmly circling her waist, palms pressed against her stomach.

"Perfect, now that you're here." She pulled away to gaze at her partner. The scar on his cheekbone glinted under the light, and she reached out to run a fingertip over it. When she asked how he got it, he explained that, the day before they met, he had accidentally cut himself while working.

He had a nervous look on his face, and it sped up her heart. But he took her garlic-scented fingers and kissed them. That immediately brought her back to normal.

As they had dinner that evening, Marcus immediately went back to the bathroom and took the ring out of its hiding place. When he passed her a glass of Pinot Grigio, she noticed there was something at nestled at the bottom of the glass. When she figured out it was a ring. Her face lit up.

"Yes!" She jumped up. "Yes!"

After that, she had no choice but to tell Marcus that she was pregnant with his child. He took the news with great joy. He had always wanted a child, and he couldn't have asked for a better mother. But they soon realized that becoming pregnant wasn't easy for every couple. A few months later, she had lost her child.

"Everything, Mama, every darn thing is perfect apart from this." Sofía sobbed into the phone. The engagement and wedding rings on her left hand taunted. They had been trying for four months after losing the baby. Nothing. She blamed herself for being on the pill for so many years. "It makes me sick," she wailed, hiccupping between words, "all those teenage girls getting pregnant by accident. What about *me*, Mama, *me*? What's wrong with me?"

"Princesita," her mother whispered, at a loss for words apart from the pet name she had been calling her daughter since she was a child.

Every morning, Sofía militantly took herbs, black cohosh, red clover, and evening primrose oil to maintain her hormones, her womb, to make her body the perfect place for her baby girl. *A girl, yes.* The knowledge that her firstborn would be a girl was sure as the recurring moon.

To Sofía's dismay, Marcus even knew what time of the month she was ovulating. The sex became routine, functionary.

"I want passion," she said to her sister on one phone-call. "It's gone."

The weight of the world became as heavy as a continent and sat on her chest, keeping her breathing shallow, her heart palpitating, and some days, it would press her to the mattress in a world of blackness. She no longer worked.

Halfway through her monthly cycle one March, her husband woke her by stroking a finger along her jawline. It was early. Robins tweeted outside. The bedroom was bright as the sun rose. He wanted her. He wanted a baby boy, Franky, named after his grandfather. When she woke, he leaned in and kissed her with so much passion, but instead he tasted salt from her tears.

"I can't," she croaked.

Marcus said goodbye at 6am. She heard the door slam; he'd gone to meet sunrise and fell trees. She imagined that it must be difficult on him too. It was weighing on both of them. Her day would pass with her on the duvet, listening to the grandfather clock chime each hour until his return when he'd cook pasta or potato.

Soon it was June, and one afternoon, Sofía had gone to the kitchen for a glass of sparkling water. She stood before the kitchen sink admiring the knives – a wedding gift from her mother in law – and slowly became aware of a yapping sound. A few moments later, a shadow coursed through the window in front of her. It was Marcus. And a tiny black puppy. A labradoodle.

Sofía called her new sour-scented puppy, "Baby."

When Baby came along, Sofía returned to life. Every morning, she'd wake with Marcus and they'd make love, slow and sensuous, and her growing dog would be heard howling downstairs for attention. When she reached the kitchen, Baby was already sitting next to her bowls, anxiously waiting to be fed. Sofía would laugh as Baby ran towards her but growled at Marcus. Baby was protective of Sofía, and Marcus was happy to see his wife pull on her trainers every morning to take the dog running along the river.

"Marcus," said Sofía one evening, walking into the living room with Baby at her heels, "my period's late."

The doctor explained that stress often contributes to infertility, and it became easier to conceive once stress is reduced or eliminated. Sure enough, along came Willow after a few months. Their pride and joy.

"Princesita," whispered Sofía when the nurse placed her into her arms.

New life. The baby they had craved so much finally crawled over the floorboards with bouncy black ringlets, almost as curly as her mother's, and of course, with her father's love of trees. It made perfect sense to name her after the type of tree she'd been conceived under, on a late balmy summer's evening when the air smelled of honeysuckle while they kept trying to shove the dog away.

Inevitably, Baby growled when Willow was around. She wasn't used to sharing Sofía's attention, and their morning runs had changed to walks, so Baby was always pulling on the lead as Sofía pushed the stroller.

"Heel, girl." Sofía abruptly yanked the lead repeatedly.

That morning, when they arrived at the park, Sofía turned away from Willow for a second to wave at a friend from her daughter's play group. A blood-curdling screech pierced the air. Sofía gasped when she turned. Willow was bleeding from the leg. Baby's paw mark. Baby growled, and for the first time, Sofía smacked Baby, who then whimpered from the pain.

Later that evening, Sofia was preparing dinner, cutting steaks on the chopping board. Marcus arrived and began whistling. He was always happy to be home after a long day of work.

Everything is perfect, he thought. Although he was still hoping for another baby, a boy this time. He gazed lovingly at his two-year-old, Willow, in the high chair. But he began to notice something. She had a wound on her leg.

"What happened?" His voice, edged in fury, demanded his wife's answer immediately.

Sofía had become used to not responding to his demands during her dark spell. She waited a moment, dishing out dinner, chips, steak, fried onions. Unusually, there were two bottles of beer on the table – open, chilled, ready. Her red nails were bright against the dark bottle as she lifted hers to meet with his glass. Marcus followed suit.

"So?"

"It was nothing." She cleared her throat and cut into her steak. "We were playing."

"It was that dog."

"That dog?" Her voice quivered, but she popped a forkful of meat into her mouth and forced a grin. Her cheeks were full as a squirrel's.

"That dog has bit me plenty of times." He pointed at scars on his arm, which she always ignored. "I don't mind being hurt, but since she hurt Willow, we'll need to put her down or send her away."

Sofía took a deep breath before placing down her cutlery. "I love Baby. She saved me when no-one else could."

They sat a moment, neither moving. Through the open window, the excited yelling of the neighbor's children could be heard as they ran up and down the street. Sofía picked up her fork and thrust it into the steak. With a mouthful, she said, "If you want to put Baby to sleep, I'll leave you. Is that what you want?"

Marcus was a little shocked his wife's words. They had never been in this type of collision before; it felt alien. But somehow, he knew that she meant it. He stood and picked up Willow. He took some anti-bacterial cream from the cabinet and moved to the living room, where he gently patted it onto his daughter's leg. The wound was a little deep, but it would heal in time. He didn't trust that dog, and until Willow was four and went off to school, he did all he could to keep them apart. Willow, of course, grew fearful of Baby and learned to avoid the dog.

"Remember the night we met?"

Whenever his wife asked that question, Marcus knew the night would end with lovemaking. They'd been together for seven years. Willow was five. She was away at his mother's, and that weekend, their passion ignited once more. A surprise came a few months later when Sofía found out she was pregnant again; they were both thrilled. Marcus was especially thrilled when the doctor told them it was going to be a boy. Not long after, little Franky was born into the world.

"Franky, you're here!" Marcus said. His dream finally came true. He cradled his son gently in the hospital room, Willow sleeping gently next to her mother.

Sofía was more confident this time. Franky was baby number two. She was ready for him. She quickly figured out what the different sounds of his crying signified, when he was hungry, tired, or needed to burp.

"Even Baby loves Franky, don't you, girl?" said Sofía, then she turned to Marcus. "She barks every time Franky drops his stuffed animal, you know?"

However, tragedy often comes when it is least expected. It happened one morning when Sofía was doing the laundry. Usually, bent in front of the washing machine, she'd be wrestling socks from Baby. When she put the last sock in, she frowned. *Where is-*

Her heart, then face, swept to the ceiling. The stairs seemed a lot longer when she scaled them, even with her unusually fast pace. There was a noise, a scuffling, and it seemed to be coming from… *NO! NO! NO!*

She ran to Franky's room. His cradle.

Her one-month old baby wasn't alone. The dog was next to him, tail wagging, nudging her baby boy's limp, bloodied body.

TWO LESS LONELY PEOPLE

"Where is it?" Chelsie Woods had practically torn her house apart trying to find her favorite lip gloss. It was a new release, and Chelsie had been on the top of the PR list. Following her YouTube review, her followers flocked the website, selling out the product before it could ever hit the shelves. "Where could it have gone?" She threw aside pillows and tore through a giant pile of laundry. "It has to be here."

She was about to return to her vanity and go through the drawers a second time when her phone buzzed with a new notification.

"Your driver, Arnel, will be arriving soon!" read the notification.

Chelsie cursed under her breath. She didn't have time to keep looking for the lip gloss, so she grabbed one of her many others and applied it just as quickly as she could. On the way to the door, she grabbed her purse and slung it over her shoulder. Sprinting down the hall, she hoped to catch the elevator. But, when she arrived, the door had already pressed itself shut. A second later, she heard the cab make its descent to the lower levels. It would take something like an eternity for it to make its way to the top floor of Chelsie's apartment building.

Her phone buzzed in her hand. "Your driver has arrived!"

With no other option, Chelsie made for the stairs, hoping that the workout videos she kept watching and following helped with her cardio. If she kept the driver waiting for too long, he was sure to drive away. Hoping to buy herself a few extra minutes, she opened the ridesharing app and sent the driver a message. "Be there in a sec."

As her thumbs flew across the keyboard, she failed to pay attention. She didn't notice the discarded soda can on the stairs. She tripped, stumbling onto the landing. Thankfully, she caught hold of the railing, righting herself before she could fall.

"Damn, that was close…" Chelsie tightened her grip on her phone for it had nearly flown from her hand. Quickly, she glanced at the screen, but thankfully, she had yet to get the notification that her driver had left. "Good."

Outside, the air was nippy. A gust of wind blew her red hair across her face, obscuring her vision. She swept it aside, and to her relief, she spotted a black sedan parked in front of the building, hazards blinking. She checked the license plate with the one listed on the app.

"It's him!" she said aloud, flailing her arms above her head to signal her approach. "Sorry to keep you waiting." She ducked inside the car and buckled herself in.

"Don't worry about it." The driver flashed a brilliant smile. "Where to?"

"Beetroot Bar & Grill," she said, checking her calendar. "I think. Just let me make sure."

"Take your time." As Arnel waited, he fiddled with the radio. "Any preference in music?"

"So long as it isn't any of the trashy pop music that they play these days," Chelsie said before suggesting a station.

"Isn't that dedicated to playing alternative rock?" asked Arnel, raising an eyebrow in question. "I never would have pegged you as the type."

"You know what they say, never judge a book by its cover." She finally found the address she was looking for and punched it into the ridesharing app. It popped up on Arnel's GPS. "Do you think we'll get caught in traffic?"

"At this hour?" Arnel reached the end of the road and took a right. "Never."

Chelsie chuckled, appreciating his sarcastic sense of humor. "At least we've got some good music to keep us entertained," she said as she leaned back, getting comfortable in her seat.

"You know, I used to love this band when I was younger. They were my first concert. It's such a shame that they broke up."

"They were my first, concert, too!" exclaimed Chelsie. "I was right there on the floor. I spent nearly every penny I had to buy those tickets."

"You're making my jealous. I would have *killed* to be on the floor, but my friends were all kind of lame back then."

"And now?"

"They are still kind of lame." He shrugged. "What about you? Meeting up with some girlfriends tonight?" They were in the thicket of LA traffic now. The highway was packed bumper to bumper. Usually, Arnel would do anything to avoid traffic, but somehow, he felt at ease being stuck in it with her.

"No, I'm actually on my way to a date with this guy who follows my YouTube channel."

"You have your own YouTube channel?" Arnel glanced over. "As a hobby or are you one of lucky few who make a living sitting in front of the camera?"

"It started as a hobby, but when it started making decent money, I decided to quit my day job at the mall and pursue it as a career. It's a lot of fun but a lot of work, too. I barely have time for a social life, even though I'm on social media almost twenty-four seven." And yet, she realized, she hadn't touched her phone since striking up a conversation with Arnel. There was just something about the driver that had captured her attention in its entirety. Perhaps it was the cut of his jaw or the dark, curly hair on the top of his head.

"That's impressive," he said, glancing her way.

The YouTuber felt her cheeks redden as her pulse quickened. Inside her chest, her heart thundered against her ribcage. There was an electrical feeling in the air, and it was growing stronger by the minute. She could barely breathe from the excitement.

Chelsie Woods had never felt like this before.

"But I have to admit, I don't use social media. I used to, but I wasn't a fan of all the hostility. People are constantly at each other's throats, and when they aren't, they're spewing political nonsense just trying to start a fight. And don't even get me started on comments." He adjusted his rearview mirror and saw a giant line of headlines trailing behind him. There was still a long way to go before reaching Chelsie's destination, but they were making good time, all things considered. "This has nothing to do with social media, but I think you're going to be a little late to your date."

"It's alright," said Chelsie. "If I was going to cancel either date, it would have been this one."

"Either date?" questioned Arnel. "Are you meeting someone else tonight?"

"I know what you're thinking, but I'm not like that. I just planned two dates on the same night like an idiot, and instead of canceling one and going through the trouble of rescheduling, I just decided to get it over with."

"You don't sound too excited to be going on these dates."

"To be honest, I'm not."

"So, why go at all?"

"As I said, I don't have much of a social life outside of work. Going on these dates seemed like a good way to get out of the house." She changed the radio station to avoid the commercials, but there was nothing else worth listening to. Realizing she would much rather talk to Arnel, she muted the volume and swiveled in her seat so she could better see the profile of his face. She didn't know whether it was the moonlight or what, but he was definitely the kind of guy she would swipe right on. "Anyway, what do you do besides drive people around?"

"I work at a juice bar. Nothing fancy. But together, these two jobs pay the bills until I can find something better. I'm actually taking online classes to become a librarian."

"A librarian?" she repeated, intrigued by the idea. "I never would have pegged you as the book-loving type."

"You know what they say." He smiled and shifted lanes to catch the exit. They were nearing Chelsie's destination, and Arnel felt a little cheated. He wanted more time with her – time to make her smile and laugh.

"So, future librarian, what kind of books do you like to read?"

"Historical fiction, mostly. I think it's fascinating how authors can spin a certain time period to fit their imagination." Arnel rattled off some of his favorites.

"You know, I haven't been to a library in a very long time. My card has probably expired by now."

"I'm sure they would be happy to renew it for you, and going to the library is a much better excuse for getting out of the house than going on a couple of dates you don't care to go to."

"You have a point," she said. "Maybe you'd want to come with me sometime? I'm sure a bookworm like you knows all the ins and outs of the LA Public Library."

"Don't tell anyone because it might cramp my style, but outside of work, I practically live there."

"So, did I just invite myself to your home? Usually, I wait for the guy to buy me dinner first."

"That can be arranged," said Arnel. "In any case, I think this is where we say our goodbyes." He pulled into an empty space and put the car into park. "It was great meeting you, Chelsie, and if you were serious about going to the library together, I'm your man." Arnel was playing up the charm, but Chelsie seemed to be ignoring him because, all of a sudden, the inside of her purse had become a lot more interesting. He rubbed the back of his neck, thinking he had been too forward with her. "But, I mean, if you don't really want to go, that's okay."

"No, no, I want to go," she mumbled, still fishing about in her purse.

Arnel was just about to ask what she was looking for when she pulled out her wallet. From it, she retrieved three crisp one-hundred-dollar bills. "I've got a proposition for you if you're willing to make a quick buck."

"I'm listening."

"Would you mind waiting for me? I don't want to get another driver who turns out to be a dud. You actually made LA traffic quite enjoyable and that's no easy feat."

He grinned. "You've got yourself a deal."

The inside of Beetroot Bar & Grill was packed. There were too many people crowding around the bar; some of them had to stand. A horrible remix was being played over the loudspeakers. The song was being blasted so loud it caused all the customers to scream at one another just to talk.

Chelsie had half a mind to turn around and save herself the headache, but before she could take a single step, someone grabbed her by the wrist, pulling her toward the nearby wall.

Jason looked just like his profile picture, but he was much taller than Chelsie expected him to be. He towered over her as he slowly pushed her until she had nowhere left to go. With her back pressed against the wall, she forced a smile onto her face. "So, uh, should we get a table?" It was unnerving her how he had yet to speak a word.

"Sure." He barreled through the crowd of people and found an empty table toward the back of the restaurant. It had a small sign that said *reserved*. A pair of sticky menus had been stuck into the napkin holder. Chelsie immediately regretted grabbing one. She realized that she had failed to replace her empty bottle of pocket hand sanitizer. For an establishment adamant about serving healthy, GMO-free food, it wasn't doing a very good job at keeping things sanitary. The condiment stand looked like it had been ransacked by a bunch of five-year-olds. But the weird thing was that no one seemed to mind. "It's awesome to finally meet you in public. I was telling my buddies at the gym that I scored a date with this super-hot YouTuber chick, but they didn't believe me. Ha!" He slapped his hand against the table.

Chelsie flinched, thinking it would break in two. Somehow, it held firm.

"Uh, thanks, I think."

An awkward silence lingered in the air, but Jason still wore a satisfied smirk on his face like he had the date in the bag. Chelsie noticed how he would keep flexing his muscles. Was that supposed to impress her? Sure, she couldn't deny that he had the body of a god, but as it stood, he seemed to have the personality of a cumquat. "Anyway, do you know what you're going to order?"

"The power bowl, obviously," he said. "It's packed with protein, and that's just what I'll need for my late-night workout."

"You're planning to work out after this?"

"Oh, definitely. I work out morning, day, and night. I live for it. You've seen my Insta, haven't you?" He took out his phone and brought up his profile.

"Come on, you've got to *work* for these kinds of results. I have a couple of clients who think they can become as swoll as me in the blink of an eye, but it just doesn't work that way."

"Right…" she said, trying not to roll her eyes.

Jason dominated the conversation, interrupting her almost every time she ventured to say something. In the end, she chose to remain silent, nibbling at the edges of her burrito bowl. For something so expensive, it wasn't worth a single penny.

He belched at the end of his meal, pounding at his chest to produce another.

Chelsie wrinkled her nose as the smell wafted across the table, insulting her sense of smell. Her stomach churned, threatening to spill whatever food she had managed to swallow. She glanced at the door, ready to get the hell out of there.

"But yeah, I'm thinking of taking the fitness coach gig to the next level. A buddy of mine is opening up a gym, and he wants me to be his business partner. Now, wouldn't that be rad?"

Rad? thought Chelsie. *If this guy keeps talking to me, I'm sure to go brain dead. I've lost some brain cells already.*

The waitress came by, chewing an obnoxious wad of gum. "Can I get you two anything else?"

"The bill, please," Chelsie said with a tone that spoke of desperation.

"And can I get you a to-go box for the rest of that burrito?"

"No, that's okay. You can just throw—" Jason interrupted by reaching across the table and snatching the rest of her food like some sort of vulture. He started chowing down with his mouth open. Apparently, this gym buff had never been taught any form of manners.

"The bill, please," Chelsie repeated.

The waitress returned with the check and a sympathetic smile. "We hope to see you again."

Chelsie wanted to say, "Never again," but she managed to hold her tongue.

Seeing as Jason seemed to have no intention of fitting the bill or even his half, Chelsie sighed and reached into her wallet, grabbing a fifty.

For the first time, Jason stopped paying attention to his food and looked straight at her – or rather, the cash she was carrying. "Looks like YouTube treats you well."

"I'm going to duck into the bathroom. Excuse me."

Jason went back to stuffing his face, and instead of going to the bathroom, Chelsie nearly ran to the parking lot, more thankful than ever that she had shelled out $300 to keep Arnel on standby.

"That bad, huh?" he said as she entered his car.

"Just get me out of here please."

Arnel drove to a nearby beach and parked with the car facing the ocean. Chelsie rolled down her window, so she could hear the soft lolling of the waves crashing against the shore. A few adrenaline seekers were catching some nighttime waves. In the distance, someone was playing music, the beat semi-decent. "I'm so glad to be out of there."

"So, what happened?"

"Oh, it was the worst. I guess it's my fault because I really did not take the time to know the guy before agreeing to meet him for a date, but he seemed nice enough. I didn't think he was going to be a blundering idiot obsessed with his own voice. He wouldn't stop talking about his workout routine and his prospects of opening a gym. I wanted to blow my brains out."

"Well, I'm really glad you didn't." Arnel rested his hand on the transmission just so it was that much closer to Chelsie's. He did not dare reach for it. Sure, he felt a connection to this girl, but did she feel the same way? Besides, he had no way of knowing whether Chelsie's second date would prove to be another bust or whether he'd sweep her off her feet. Arnel was going to play it safe – for now.

She sighed. "Mind if we take a small walk on the beach? I have a bit of time before I need to meet up with Bobby."

"Sure, I don't mind." Arnel was out of his seat and rounding the car. He opened Chelsie's door for her with a dazzling smile.

"Are you always this much of a gentleman?" she asked.

"Only to the customers who tip me well," he said with a wink.

"Oh, so this is just about the tip, is it?"

Arnel held out his arm. "It can be a little tricky getting down to the beach. Make sure you don't fall."

"Unfortunately, being a klutz is something of a specialty of mine."

"We can stay in the car –"

"No," she interrupted. "Just don't let me go."

"I won't." Carefully, they climbed down the rock wall until Arnel was safely at the bottom, shoes sinking into the sand. "Jump, I'll catch you."

"Jump?" questioned Chelsie. "Are you sure I should be doing that? I don't want to show up to my second date with a twisted ankle."

"Trust me."

Chelsie really had no reason to trust the driver, and yet as soon as she looked into his smoldering eyes, she felt her inhibitions melt away. With a small scream, she plunged forward, caught by a pair of capable arms. Arnel was nowhere as muscled as Jason had been, but he was lean with a body that spoke of healthy habits.

He steadied her. "See?" His hands fell to her hips. He wasn't even thinking about it, but it sent a shudder through Chelsie's spine because it made her realize how close they were standing – nearly chest to chest. If he took just another step towards her, he would no doubt feel the erratic beating of her heart.

She reminded herself to breathe, but just as soon as she filled her lungs, she was hit with a scent stronger than the salt lingering in the air. It took Chelsie only a moment to realize that it was *him*. It wasn't quite cologne. His body wash, maybe? Whatever it was, Chelsie liked it. She found herself leaning forward, trying to figure out exactly what it reminded her of.

Arnel was surprised to find Chelsie moving in, eyes closed, lips slightly puckered. *Is she going to kiss me right now?* he thought, wanting desperately for her to open her eyes just so he could see the stars twinkling in their depths.

"Aha!" she exclaimed suddenly. "A rain forest, that's what you smell like."

"Excuse me?" Arnel furrowed his brow. "I think I missed something. What about the rain forest?"

"You smell like one."

"I do?" Arnel lifted his shirt to his nose.

Chelsie chuckled. "What kind of body wash do you use?"

"I don't really pay attention to that sort of stuff. I just grab whatever is showcased at the end of the aisle to save me the hassle of choosing from a million different brands. Really, I don't know how you women do it because I've seen the beauty aisle and that, to me, is what nightmares are made of. How do you ever decide what to buy?"

"Why do you think it always takes us forever to do our shopping?" Chelsie found it so easy to laugh when she was with Arnel. He made her feel weightless, like all her usual problems were no longer so important. Unlike when she filmed, she didn't feel the need to put on an act. She could just be herself.

Together, they reached the water. Chelsie took off her shoes and felt the sand between her toes. "You know, I'm almost tempted to cancel my date with Bobby to stay here on the beach."

"What's stopping you?"

"He's the son to one of my dad's golf buddies, and my dad will not get off my case until I give him a chance. I managed to hold out for a little while, but I just can't take my dad nagging me anymore. And who knows? Maybe he's the guy I've been waiting for."

Arnel managed to keep the disappointment from his face. "I hope all goes well for you, then. From what I've seen, you seem like you deserve the best."

She rested her hand on his arm. "You're too nice, Arnel." She sat down and hugged her knees against her chest. "Your girlfriend is very lucky to have you."

"My girlfriend?" It was his turn to laugh. "I haven't had a girlfriend in a few years."

"Oh?"

He shrugged and joined Chelsie. "I guess I've had my fair share of bad romances, and I'm just waiting for someone worth the time."

"What kind of girl would be worth your time?" asked Chelsie.

Someone like you, Arnel wanted to say, but before he could answer her with some generic response, her phone dinged with a new notification. Arnel lost her to whatever was written on the screen.

"I should probably be getting you to that second date. I wouldn't want you to be late twice in a row." He helped her up and then together, they scaled the rock wall, making it back to the car in one piece. "Where to this time?"

"It's not far from here. It's called the Rocky Cove Café and Fishery."

"Isn't that the one where you can order a fishing rod off the menu and throw it off the deck?"

"That's the one. Bobby opened it right after high school."

"How did he manage that?"

"With a small loan from his father," answered Chelsie. "His father owns a chain of burger joints, so I guess he wanted Bobby to follow in his footsteps."

"Ah."

"Yeah. Don't you think that's pretty cool?"

"Yeah. It's pretty cool," he said. "Maybe I'll go there sometime when I'm not working." Arnel kept his eyes fixed on the road as he kept driving.

He felt his shoulders begin to sag. How was he supposed to compete with a guy who owns one of the coolest cafés in town? There was always a line of people waiting to get in. That alone was bound to get Chelsie's attention. Arnel had a feeling that Chelsie would come out of her second date thinking she had scored herself a home run. And maybe she would. Who was Arnel to get in the way of that?

"Well, I would leave you at the door, but that parking lot is packed. Would you mind if I just pulled over here?"

"Not at all." Chelsie seemed eager to get out of the car as she quickly unbuckled herself. "Thanks again – for everything." She handed over a little bit extra, adding to the $300 she had already paid him.

Arnel shook his head. "$300 was more than enough, Chelsie. Now, go in there and enjoy yourself. From what you told me about date number one, this one is bound to be a thousand times better."

"You think?" She returned her wallet to her purse and checked her makeup in the side mirror. Clearly, she wanted to impress this Bobby fellow, and who could blame her? She had known a few of the girls who went to high school with him, and he was that one boy everyone wanted to be with. "Anyway, thanks again, Arnel. I'll be sure to leave a raving review." And with that, she was gone.

Arnel kept his car idle as he booted up the ridesharing app on his app, planning to pick up someone else, but then he shook his head. "No," he said aloud. "I'm waiting." Something about Chelsie had struck him – reaching down to his very core. It was the sort of spark he had read about in countless novels. He never thought it could be real, yet he could feel it pulsating through every vein in his body, and he just couldn't ignore it.

As Chelsie approached the restaurant, she was pleasantly surprised. A live band was setting up for the night and their choice of instruments promised something good. As she walked toward the entrance, she spotted Bobby instantly. He was leaning against the wall like he was posing for some 50s magazine. There was a boyish grin on his face as soon as he saw Chelsie walking his way. He met her halfway and captured her in a hug.

Chelsie felt the butterflies swarming in her stomach, but for some reason, an image of Arnel crossed her mind.

"I'm glad you could make it." He flashed another boyish grin before grabbing her hand. "I heard you were a fan of alternative rock, so I took the liberty of hiring a band I thought you might like."

"Really?"

"Of course," he whispered against her ear. "I always aim to impress." Without another hesitation, he slipped his arm around her waist. "How about a drink?"

"Sure."

Chelsie considered the blackboard menu. "What would you recommend?"

"Our Irish Coffee is a best seller."

"It's alcoholic?"

"It is," he confirmed. "Is that a problem?"

"I don't really drink on first dates. It's nothing against you, just a way to keep myself accountable." She saw a glimmer of disappointment cross his features, but they disappeared in the blink of an eye, replaced by an unmistakable confidence. "I think I'll just have a tea latte."

"Not a problem." He ordered their drinks. "And I have to respect your decision not to drink on a first date. There are some crazy people out there. I don't blame you for wanting to stay safe."

"Thank you." Chelsie smiled. "So, about that band. Do you always have live music on the weekend or did you make a special exception just for me? Because I find that hard to believe."

"Maybe if you stick around long enough, you'll find out." He grabbed his drink and set off toward the deck. There was an empty table with two fishing rods set against the railing. "I know your father golfs, but do you fish?"

"Can't say I've ever tried."

"That's about to change."

"This is going to end disastrously."

"Don't worry. I'm here." Bobby was behind her, arms reaching around to grab the fishing rod. He adjusted her grip. "You want to release the line here, and then you pull back and let it fly." His words were like honey. "And when you feel a nibble, you pull up to sink the hook and start reeling. That's the short and sweet of it." The bobber was carried along the waves, disappearing for a brief moment before reappearing again. Chelsie tried to focus on that little blob of red, but it was extremely difficult when Bobby continued to press his body against her back, hands still clasped around hers.

"So, I have to admit that I've seen a few of your videos, and you're really quite good. There's been a few times when I was tempted to go out and buy some highlighter."

"You're kidding."

"Have you seen my cheekbones?"

Chelsie turned her head to look. As she did so, her lips came dangerously close to those of her date's. There was a sparkle in Bobby's eye that made Chelsie think that he had intended it that way.

Suddenly, Chelsie felt a nibble at the end of her line. She yanked the rod as Bobby had instructed. Doing so, she whacked him accidentally, narrowly missing his nose. He stumbled backward, holding his forehead.

"Sorry!" Chelsie dropped the rod and ran to his side. The fish, now hooked, pulled on the line.

Bobby caught the end of the rod before it could fly off the deck. "Go on, reel it in," he prompted.

"But are you alright? I managed to hit you hard enough to leave a mark." Chelsie frowned. "Let me get you some ice or something."

"I'll be fine," he insisted. "A little bump on the head isn't going to kill me. Besides, I'm not going to have you miss out on your first ever catch on my account." He placed the rod in her hand and offered a smile of encouragement.

Chelsie was hesitant, but once she felt the fish fighting the line, she began to reel. It was much harder than she thought. Whatever she had hooked, it was big enough to bend the tip of the rod until it nearly touched the water.

"This thing is going to snap!" she said, planting her heels into the wooden deck. She wasn't about to let a fish get the best of her.

Sweat gathered at her upper lip. The muscles of her arm felt strained, but she wasn't going to make a fool of herself. So far, she was enjoying her time with Bobby. The last thing she wanted was for him to think that she was weak.

"Careful, now." He grabbed her by the hips and steadied her. "Here, let me help." Again, his lips were against her ear, whispering softly. His hand took hold of hers, guiding her through the motions. With his help, it became easier.

"I think I see it," said Chelsie as a flash of silver shot just underneath the surface of the water. Her excitement gave her a temporary boost of strength. She braced herself against Bobby's body and brought in her catch.

Bobby whistled. "That's a good one – biggest one of the month. We'll have to get it measured and put your name on the wall of fame."

"What do you do with the fish after its measured?"

"We throw it back into the water, so it can return to its family."

Chelsie was thankful for that. She was a big fan of sushi, but she didn't think she could bring herself to eat something she had brought to its end with her own hands.

"So, did I make it into the record books?" Chelsie rose to the tips of her toes to see over Bobby's shoulder as he measured the fish.

"Sixteen inches." He whistled again. "You nearly took my throne with this one, but I'm still reigning as king with an 18-incher."

"Isn't it a little unfair to be counting the fish caught by the café's owner?" she asked. "For all I know, you could be back here all night just trying for the biggest catch."

"Perhaps, but do I really seem like a dishonest guy?"

Chelsie dared to take the fish from his hand. It was slimy, and when it started moving, she nearly screamed. Somehow, she managed to maintain her hold and throw it over the railing. With a plunk, the fish disappeared into the water's depths.

"There's a sink right over there if you want to wash your hands. In fact, I'd recommend it. You don't want to smell like tuna all night."

When Chelsie had finished scrubbing her hands raw, she joined Bobby at the table. He had his drink in his hand, sipping casually. His eyes followed her as she took a seat. There was a certain hunger to them that Chelsie could not quite understand. It made her just the slightest bit uneasy, but she chose to ignore it, wanting instead to enjoy her night with Bobby. "If I had known I would have this much fun coming here, I would have scheduled a date sooner."

"I'm glad you like it here. The door is always open."

"This latte is fantastic, by the way. Now I know why there's always a line to get into this place. I could die for this."

Bobby laughed. "You flatter me, but I would prefer it if you stayed alive. If you die tonight, when am I supposed to see you again?"

"You want to see me again?" Chelsie felt herself blush. She had to admire Bobby for getting straight to the point, but it still took her by surprise. Sure, she was having a good time, but she felt like something was missing somehow – what that something was, Chelsie could not quite figure out, but it nagged at the edges of her mind.

She was drawn forward by Bobby's impish smile, wanting to know more about him and how he came to have an idea for his fishing café.

"We were visiting some family in Virginia Beach, and we rented some property over there. The deck was just like this one, and the owner had left his rods in the garage for us to use. I came to love the combination of coffee and casting a line, so I decided to bring the idea back to California. As you can tell, it's been a smashing success. I've already gotten a few offers for franchising, but I'm not sure I want to share my little slice of paradise with anyone else. There comes a certain novelty with owning the only fishing café in town."

Chelsie listened to his every word, but when her phone buzzed with a notification feed, she found herself checking it.

"What about you?" he asked, trying to recapture her attention. "How did you get into YouTubing?"

"It started as a hobby, and it just took off. I never imagined it would become a lucrative career, but hey, I'm not complaining."

"I noticed you don't wear a lot of makeup. And I mean that in the best way. With a face like yours, there's nothing worth hiding." Bobby was smooth with his compliments, and he knew it. When his smile deepened, Chelsie saw his dimples for the first time. Somehow, he was getting cuter by the minute, and she didn't know whether she could handle it.

"Are you always this nice?"

"Only to the girls I want to share a dance with." He held out his hand in invitation.

Chelsie took it, charmed by all his flirting. It had been such a long time since Chelsie had gone on a date with a decent guy. Maybe her dad had been right to nag her. She had been missing out all this time. "I have to warn you. I'm not the best dancer."

"Don't worry." He took her by the waist and spun her so she hung at the tips of his fingers suspended like a ballerina. "Just follow my lead." He reeled her back and pressed his hand against it, locking her hips against his. In a blur of motion, they joined the rest of the crowd who were already dancing.

Chelsie tried to keep track of what was happening, but it was all rushing past her. Every second, someone new bumped into her. Apologizing proved impossible over the sound of the music. The dance floor seemed to surge as a new crowd of people joined the growing mosh pit.

"Uh, I don't know if I'm comfortable being here. I get rather anxious in big crowds of people." She scanned all that was around her, looking for a means of escape, but every direction was blocked off by a wall of people. "Bobby, let go of me please. I need some air."

"Relax," he whispered, voice husky. His hand was no longer on the small of her back. It had ventured much lower than that. "You're getting all worked up for nothing. I thought we were having a good time." Before she could realize what was happening, he had her against the back wall. "Trust me, stick around, and I'll make sure you enjoy every pleasure the night has to offer."

Chelsie saw his hand reaching for her chest. So, being a nice guy had just been an act. Typical. She should have known. Guys like Bobby are always too good to be true. They only want one thing, and Chelsie wasn't going to give it to him. Maybe he had scored this way in the past, but he wasn't going to score tonight. Chelsie would make sure of it.

With fury blazing through every feature of her face, she slapped the café owner. She had honed all her strength into the blow, praying it would hurt because she wasn't the kind of girl to take a guy's piggish intentions sitting down. "Don't you dare touch me," she growled, jabbing a finger into his chest. "You had me thinking you were a nice guy, but the gig is up. I'm out of here."

"Don't be like this. I'm sorry."

"I'm sorry?" Chelsie spoke through her teeth. "Do you really think that's going to be good enough? I don't even know you and you're already trying to cop a feel. Let me tell you something, buddy, that won't fly with me."

Arnel had managed to snag a spot near the entrance. He kept an eye on the door, but even after an hour, there was no sign of Chelsie. He tilted his head back and closed his eyes.

Why had he even bothered waiting? Clearly, whoever this Bobby guy was, he was showing Chelsie a good time. Had the date crashed and burned like the first one, she would have come running out of the café by now.

The band finished a song and rolled straight into another. Even from the car, the acoustics were amazing. Arnel could only imagine what it must sound like from the inside.

Arnel watched the door for a few minutes more, but all he saw were a few drunken couples making their way to the parking lot. He could only hope they weren't the ones driving. Just in case, he waited until they were gone before turning on the engine. The radio competed with the live music. Arnel turned it off before the clash of sounds gave him a headache.

The clock glowed a bright green light. It was really time for him to be heading back. With work in the morning, he needed to get some sleep.

He half-expected Chelsie to come running out any minute, but that was just wishful thinking.

He decided that she probably never would. He put the car in reverse. He checked the rearview mirror to make sure there wasn't anyone behind his car. Arnel was just about to pull out of the space when he saw her. She had this frantic look on her face. Something had happened. His grip tightened on the steering wheel as anger soured in his mouth, but that didn't matter. First and foremost, he had to make sure she was truly okay. Quickly, he shifted into park and got out of the car, running to her side.

"Arnel?" Chelsie couldn't believe it. "I thought you had left. What are you still doing here?"

"I wanted to make sure you had a getaway driver."

She threw her arms around him and buried her face in his shoulder. "I'm so glad you're here," she whispered, taking comfort in the earthiness of his scent. Having him near made her feel rooted – safe.

"What happened?" he asked, gently tilting her chin so he could see her face.

She shook her head. "Let's just get out of here. If I never see this place again, it will be too soon."

Respecting her boundaries, Arnel did not press the issue any further. Seeing as she was shaking, he shrugged off his jacket and pressed it around her. "Come on. Let's get you home." He opened her door and helped her inside.

Once they were on the road, he turned on the heat. Once again, they were caught in traffic. His phone alerted him of an accident up ahead. "Looks like we'll be stuck here a while."

"I don't mind if it means I'm with you." Chelsie slipped her arms into the jacket. It was oversized, but she didn't mind. It smelled just like Arnel, and at that moment, she wanted to be deep in the rainforest because everywhere else had turned out to be a total nightmare. "I really cannot thank you enough for sticking around. Had I needed to wait for another driver, there was no telling what could have happened." Chelsie shuddered to think of facing Bobby after what he had tried to do. She squeezed her eyes shut just to force the thought from her mind. "I'm glad you're not like that," whispered Chelsie, more to herself than to Arnel.

"Hmm?"

"I just can't believe it. I mean, the nerve of that guy."

Arnel looked over and saw Chelsie had her hands balled into fists. Wanting to calm her down, he reached over and fitted his fingers through hers. "Whatever happened, don't let it ruin your night." He squeezed her hand lightly. "Because, whoever this Bobby guy is, he isn't worth your time if he's succeeded in upsetting you after a first date." He went to remove his hand, but Chelsie held on, wanting to feel the warmth of his hand.

"Thank you."

"You don't have to thank me for telling the truth." Arnel inched forward. Seeing that the next exit was open, he decided to get off the highway. "And I know I said I would take you home, but there's a really amazing ice cream shop not too far from here." He smiled. "And if you ask me, there's nothing better at cheering someone up than a cone of vanilla ice cream."

"Vanilla?" quipped Chelsie. "Everyone knows chocolate is a thousand times better."

Arnel shook his head, clicking his tongue against the roof of his mouth like someone disappointed. "I don't think this is going to work. I definitely can't be seen with you at the library if you think chocolate ice cream is the better of the two." He tried to keep a straight face, but as soon as he heard Chelsie laughing, he laughed alongside her.

"Can we agree to disagree and we can both have some twists?"

"Rainbow sprinkles?" asked Arnel.

"They are called jimmies, but yes."

"You're really drawing a line in the sand here."

"Maybe I'm just waiting for you to cross over to my side," she grinned. The playful tug and pull of their conversation made her forget all about what had happened between her and Bobby. Arnel was right. Chelsie was only wasting her time getting upset over the lowlife. There were better men to focus on.

They arrived at the ice cream parlor. Arnel parked in the back. He rounded the car and opened Chelsie's door, holding out his hand.

She took it.

Arnel hoisted her to her feet with the utmost ease. Maybe pulling just a little too hard, their bodies collided. All of a sudden, their faces were inches apart. Both their hearts quickened with intentions that had formed from the very start. Arnel itched to cup her face in his hand and kiss her, but he would take things slowly – savor every moment. If he was lucky, they would have plenty of time to do such things. For tonight, all he wanted to do was get to know the girl that had invaded his thoughts all night.

"Come on. Let's go get that ice cream." He thought she would let go of his hand, but she laced her fingers against his. The tops of her cheeks became rosy. Arnel smiled.

Hand in hand, they joined the line.

"I know we agreed on getting twists, but I didn't know this place made all their own ice cream. It almost seems like a crime to get a cone. I'm thinking a couple of scoops of cookies and cream. What do you think?"

"You can never go wrong with cookies and cream, but the rocky road is pretty good."

"Maybe we can get both and share?" she suggested.

"That sounds like a fantastic idea. Best of both worlds."

"Exactly."

They found themselves a table. "Do you want the cherry?"

"You can have it," said Chelsie. "I don't care for cherries."

Arnel shook his head. "You know, you're making it really hard for me to like you."

"And yet you waited."

"I was hoping that the third time's the charm." He rubbed the back of his hand, a little embarrassed by his response. "Is that too forward of me?"

"No," said Chelsie. "Because I'm hoping that the third time's the charm, too." With that thought, she took her first bite of ice cream, and it had never tasted so sweet.

9 780578 749112